25

BEYOND THE BONE

Recent Titles by Reginald Hill from Severn House

BEYOND THE BONE
THE LOW ROAD
MATLOCK'S SYSTEM
THE TURNING OF THE TIDE
SINGLETON'S LAW

BEYOND THE BONE

Reginald Hill

This title first published in Great Britain 2000 by
SEVERN HOUSE PUBLISHERS LTD of
9–15 High Street, Sutton, Surrey SM1 1DF.
Originally published in 1975 under the title *Urn Burial*
and pseudonym of *Patrick Ruell.*
This title first published in the USA 2000 by
SEVERN HOUSE PUBLISHERS INC., of
595 Madison Avenue, New York, NY 10022,

British Library Cataloguing in Publication Data

Hill, Reginald, 1936-
    Beyond the bone
    1.   Cumbria (England) - Fiction
    2.   Detective and mystery stories
    I.   Title
    823.9'14 [F]

    ISBN 0-7278-5510-7

Printed and bound in Great Britain by
MPG Books Ltd, Bodmin, Cornwall.

FOREWORD

THE PRICE OF a hardback novel has always been similar to the cost of a meal. Because Patrick Ruell and I have enjoyed some memorable repasts, I found myself thinking of good food as I savoured this book.

The *aperitif* is, of course, the reputation and literary skill of Patrick Ruell, otherwise known as Reginald Hill. He is one of Britain's foremost crime writers with some thirty novels to his credit. Like any aperitif selected as the precursor to a feast, so the reputation of this writer is such that we know beyond all doubt that we are going to relish what follows.

Like a starter with indefinable flavours, is this a bouquet of modern times or is there a hint of something more exotic? Even at an early stage, can we sense a delicate sapor of bygone or mystical times? We cannot be too sure even if our apparently simple but very pleasurable experience begins at Brampton.

This is a tiny market town in North Cumbria wherein lie the offices of the North East Cumberland Development Council. It's an ordinary place full of ordinary people doing ordinary things. Thus we might be tempted into believing we are about to enjoy an ordinary dish. Sam Lakenheath, chief officer of that council, has to persuade expanding companies to make use of the derelict site of a former research centre on Thirlsike Waste in the nearby hills. But the ordinary changes to the extraordinary as our taste buds become excited by the stormy arrival of a huge and angry young woman called Zeugma Gray.

Her guardian is the eminent but enigmatic archaeologist, Professor Leo Pasquino. As we savour this course, we learn that the research centre has, in the recent past, been used for the secretive development of a missile fuel. But once again, those subtle and perhaps indefinable flavours of the past emerge because this complex, part of which was once an old fever hospital, is built on the site of a Bronze Age urn field. As we head for the main course, there is a hint of savoury seasonings; a former research director of that establishment was found hanging in a Californian motel, Professor Pasquino disappears and so does an 1800 year old Roman skeleton he has discovered. Puzzling and pungent relish can be scented at this stage and, just like a rich meal comprising several choice ingredients, we are told of an urn containing a curious white powder and of Zeugma's former lover, Hasan bin Radhaur, who arrives on the scene bearing the name of Malcolm Upas.

Mystery gives way to drama with the untimely death of a man in a blazing car. Lakenheath realises that the car might have been his and that he might have been driving it at that moment, and this reminds him of a falling rock which almost killed him on another occasion . . . We tuck into this course as the tension increases; the meal is now giving forth its full potential but there are some wondrous moments to come. And yet there persists a tantalising mystery—we are never quite sure what we are tasting, we cannot quite identify the aroma.

But the meal is of such exquisite mouth-watering appeal that we continue, hoping that the source of all those magic flavours will be revealed. Who is the mysterious Crow, a man who races across the fells against his wolf-like dog? It was Crow who found the body of a recently murdered girl; it is Crow who guards his remote cottage with a bird of prey while a hare (a witch hare?) appears from time to time as if scrutinising all visitors.

But throughout our feast, there is the sinister presence of the old research centre with its underground compartments; and what is the fate of the hippies who stayed here? Who is the mysterious man called Diss? As we attempt to identify all the tastes upon our palate, the ebullient Zeugma becomes our pepsin as she charges through the labyrinth of story strands.

With the delectations of main course locked in our memories, we turn with epicurean desire to the sweet. If this fully complements the earlier portions of the meal, it will long live in our memories and so it does through the dramatic and

fulfilling climax to this novel. The book provides a very satis-
fying feast but good food needs a good wine, and good wines
contain many abstruse scents. And who can positively identify all that is contained in the finest wine or food?

There are hidden secrets in this book; like any good meal,
we want to savour it again. It will never quite be the same
though; with every reading, there will always be some new
discovery to intrigue us.

PETER N. WALKER

Peter N. Walker, a policeman for thirty years, retired in 1982
to write full-time. He is author of more than eighty books, fact
and fiction, including many crime novels. His latest is *Grave
Secrets*, published by Constable. His best known titles are the
'Constable' books, written as Nicholas Rhea, which inspired
the hugely successful ITV series 'Heartbeat'. In May 1992 he
was elected to the Committee of the Crime Writers' Associ-
ation and is secretary of its Northern Chapter.

For David and Cheryl

Beside, to preserve the living, and make the dead to live, to keep men out of their Urnes, and discourse of humane fragments in them, is not impertinent to our profession; whose study is life and death, who daily behold examples of mortality, and of all men least need artificial mementos, or coffins by our bedside, to mind us of our graves.

SIR THOMAS BROWNE: Urne Buriall

Urne Buriall, a discourse on an urn-field uncovered in Norfolk and a meditation on the meaning of death, was written by Sir Thomas Browne in 1658. All the chapter headings are taken from this work.

I

To be ignorant of evils to come, and forgetfull of evils past, is a mercifull provision in nature . . .

The wind poured out of the east that night, a chilling torrent which penetrated every nook and cranny of the ancient wall so that there was no lee to the north or to the south as its waves scoured the gorge of the Irthing and roared in triumph over the broken walls of the once mighty fort at Camboglanna. Not many of the living moved in the waste that night, but a few there were and they felt the storm's fury for a while.

Crow stirred uneasily in the narrow confines of the straw-filled niche which served as his bed. In the low-roofed chamber lit only by the dying embers of a peat fire, the creatures which shared his dwelling woke instantly to bright-eyed awareness. Crow's eyes too were open but he saw nothing of the room nor of the attendant beasts. Instead images crowded into his mind, misty, confused, overlapping, so that there was no way of separating past, present and future, if indeed they were more than the meaningless fragments of fantasy each man carries beneath his diurnal thoughts.

He saw men in their fury and terror slaying other men; spears splitting linked armour and short swords slicing through animal fells; he saw other men killing for other needs; saw a girl's mouth open in a scream which only pleasured those who heard it; saw a man swing at a rope's end, his black tongue deriding those who lived on; saw a raging fire which devoured and purified; saw a naked woman come close with death in her eyes; saw an urn full of the ashes of many lives, many hopes; and saw himself buried deep in a cavern from which only his despairing cries could ever escape.

He shook his head and broke up the images, lay in thought for a while, then fell into a deep and untroubled sleep while outside the wind drove the thin wiry moorgrass in waves of panic over the contours of the indifferent land.

2

*But who knows the fate of his bones, or
how often he is to be buried?*

It was just past noon on a March day washed clean by
wind and showers that Zeugma found the first skeleton.

'Good,' she said. 'Super,' as she started to brush the
dirt out of the empty eye-socket.

'I say, well done, Humpty,' said her companion, peering
appreciatively into the trench. 'Look, I've poured myself
a mug of coffee. Do you want one now or can't you drag
yourself away?'

She thought for a moment, running her earth-stained
fingers absently along the smooth curve of the skull's
cheek-bones.

'All right,' she said. 'I'll break for lunch. If I don't,
you'll just eat all the smoked salmon and leave me the
cheese. Give us a hand up. And don't call me Humpty.'

He reached into the trench and pulled her out. They
stood close for a moment; the man, Leo Pasquino, tall,
gangling, middle-aged, his expression of amiable
vacancy accentuated by the unseeing blankness of his left
eye which was made of glass; the girl in her middle twen-
ties, unambiguously plump, her rosy cheeks glowing
through an unrestrainable tangle of russet hair. Recently
someone had told her she looked like a personification of
Keats' autumn. As he had been attempting to unzip her
slacks at the time, she assumed it was a compliment.

9

Behind them the treeless moorland ran away in rising undulations as though eager to reach a horizon which seemed to press close against the faded blue-wash of the sky.

Pasquino turned and made his way to a dust-caked Range Rover on the bonnet of which rested a picnic hamper. Zeugma stayed a little longer, meditatively returning the empty stare from the broken earth below.

'Come on,' called her companion. 'He's been there eighteen hundred years. I don't suppose he's going anywhere now.'

'No, I don't suppose he is,' she said, turning.

At the Range Rover, the man was busily thrusting smoked salmon sandwiches into his mouth two at a time. The cheese, she noted, were quite untouched.

'After we've eaten,' he said in a muffled voice, 'I think I'll stroll up to the top there and do a bit of surveying. You don't get much of this weather up here and I should be able to do a visual check of these aerial photos.'

'I thought the camera couldn't lie,' said Zeugma.

'True, but like most things incapable of dishonesty, it can't think either. Even one human eye perched before an expert and experienced human brain is worth a hundred Leicas.'

'Still, we wouldn't be here if it wasn't for the camera,' she answered, her own voice muffled now as she made sure that at least she got her fair share of the cheese. 'It was lucky you got hold of those photos.'

'They merely help to confirm what I know,' he said, as if piqued. 'Well, I'll be off. Watch how you go now. He was doubtless a brave chap. Give him a decent resurrection. See you in about an hour.'

He gulped down a final mouthful of the filthy black coffee he always took with him on his expeditions to the Great Outdoors. It was deliberately made as strong and bitter as possible to discourage others from sharing it, but

Zeugma had trained herself to stomach the stuff. It was, she claimed, a necessary survival technique.

Thrusting the flask and the last two smoked salmon sandwiches into a small rucksack which he draped casually over his left shoulder, he set off north and uphill, waving his two-and-a-half-inch Ordnance Survey map in a gesture which may have been valedictory or merely an effort to unfold it.

Zeugma watched him for a while, then with a bit of a sigh she stepped carefully into the trench. No doubt Leo would return in an hour or two having made half a dozen discoveries more important than her own excavation. But her own researches had brought her here and in fairness he had been most co-operative. She regarded the bones at her feet with a feeling of strong possessiveness.

Pasquino knelt in the damp grass and looked with interest at the object he had just unearthed. To the untutored eye it was an urn, but he recognized it as a bell beaker of the early Bronze Age. It was not empty. Carefully he inserted his hand and examined with interest the fine white powder which adhered to his fingers. Whistling tunelessly to himself, he now pursued his excavations with something less than the meticulous care he preached to his disciples. Indeed one or two more artefacts he unearthed and put aside in a fashion almost cavalier until the small trenching tool struck through the earth at the main object of his search. Now he used his fingers until sufficient soil had been removed to confirm his find.

For a few moments he sat back on his heels, rocking gently to and fro as his mind examined the possible procedures to be followed. It may have been seconds or minutes before he realized he was being watched.

The young man who stood behind him smiled uncertainly as though in half recognition.

'Professor Pasquino, is it?' he said.

'Yes,' said Pasquino.

'I thought it was,' said the young man with relief and came forward with his hand outstretched.

'Access? No problem, Mr Bulstrode. We'd get top priority for something like this. We could turn that little winding road into a four-lane highway in no time at all.'

Sam Lakenheath spoke with all the authority of the chief officer of the North East Cumberland Development Council. And where this high position did not win automatic respect, his appearance was always ready to give a nudge in the right direction.

At thirty (arguably the age where youthful vigours and mature thought find their most productive union) he was still athletically slim. His hair was cut at just the right length to avoid being offensive to either trendy visitors from the south or his local bare-necked employers. And he dressed well, suiting himself admirably for each occasion; but just well enough to excite admiration, never envy.

His companion, a shiny middle-aged man in a lightweight suit, slowly turned through 360 degrees, scanning the surrounding countryside intensely as though imprinting every contour on his mind. For a moment Lakenheath felt the stirrings of hope.

Bulstrode spoke.

'There's a potential here, certainly, Mr Lakenheath. I'd like to stay on for a couple of days, up to the weekend perhaps, and really get some kind of feel of the area. What we've got to remember is, if Poly-fibre moved up here, it's not just a question of plant and siting, no, it's a question of shifting a substantial number of our executives. And would they come? That's one of the things the board will want my comments on. Recreational facilities, that kind of thing. What's the night life like? How would we be fixed for getting into the golf club? That kind of thing. There is a golf club, isn't there?'

'Several,' said Lakenheath. The note of vibrant enthusiasm had faded from his voice. He had been here before; he recognized the symptoms. Before his very eyes he had seen Bulstrode, Proteus-like, change shape. Poly-fibre-man, recognizable by his keen eyes, his slightly flared nostrils and his functional, uncluttered silhouette, had disappeared; and with him any chance of Poly-fibre bringing a new age of prosperity to East Cumberland. In his place was Bulstrode-man with three days to kill and someone else paying all expenses. To the imaginative eye his silhouette now had a golf bag on its shoulders, a glass at his lips and something like Mr Punch's truncheon protruding from its loins.

'Miss Amis!' called Bulstrode.

'Yes?' Bulstrode's secretary rose languidly from the grassy bank on which she had been enjoying the sunshine. Upright she swayed uncertainly like a new-born calf on long elegant legs. Even in motion, thought Lakenheath gloomily, she finds it hard to keep them together.

'Time to go, Miss Amis. Lots to do. We'll be staying on a couple of days.'

'Oh,' said Miss Amis, making only a token effort to sound surprised.

'Shall we go?'

Without waiting for an answer, Bulstrode set off down the rutted track which led back to the road. Lakenheath glanced round one more time and shrugged his shoulders. He was really neither disappointed nor surprised, though something competitive in him prevented him from ever just going through the motions. But it was hard to imagine anything less like a factory site than this slow, powerful surge of land, almost unchanged in contour and vegetation since the Romans patrolled its heights, doubtless wondering what the hell they were doing so far from home. Only the distant roofs of the cottages forming the tiny hamlet of Blackrigg gave evidence that time had passed, and their architecture, organic rather than cerebral, had nothing to do with concrete and glass.

Never mind the Romans, what am I doing here? wondered Lakenheath as he set off after Miss Amis whose far from sensible sandals were setting up a wobble which reached all the way to her behind. Lakenheath fixed his eyes on this interesting phenomenon and quickened his pace slightly.

I'm wasting my time here, his thoughts drifted on. *What can I hope to achieve? Best to forget it and get out with dignity while I can. Enjoy yourself!*

He caught up with Miss Amis. Bulstrode was almost out of sight. A man must take his chances. *At my back I always hear Time's winged chariot hurrying near.* He placed his hand at the base of Miss Amis's spine and said, 'Are you all right, my dear?'

She smiled at him, but now a new sound joined the rustle of wind and cry of birds. It came from behind and he thought again, this time with alarm, of Time's winged chariot.

But when he turned he saw that Time was travelling in a hard-driven Range Rover and clearly had no intention of stopping.

He glimpsed a round rosy face mouthing inaudible suggestions at him, then he and Miss Amis subsided into a hawthorn bush in what, in other circumstances and vegetation, might have been an interesting tangle of limbs. Angrily and unchivalrously he pushed himself upright and set off down the track vowing vengeance on the Range Rover's driver.

His chance came sooner than expected. He had left the ancient Morris Oxford which the N.E.C.D.C. generously let him use on its official business parked in the neck of the track, just off the minor road which ran down to Blackrigg. To attempt to bring it further would have been suicidal. It was blocking the Range Rover's access to the road, however, and the female driver, a wild figure with dishevelled hair and a plump body which threatened every seam of her cotton blouse and denim slacks, was haranguing Bulstrode.

'Either you move this museum-piece or I will! Do you think you own the blasted road or something. For heaven's sake, man, don't stand there like a fossilized frog. Move the car!'

Despite his own anger, Lakenheath found he got a small charge of pleasure from hearing Bulstrode so addressed.

He joined the fray.

'This is my car. What seems to be the trouble?'

'Well, if it's your car, *you* move the damned thing.' She had a strong, girls' public school kind of voice.

'Would you mind telling ...'

'Look. You're inconsiderate, we've established that. I hope to heaven you're not going to turn out to be stupid as well. I want to get out on the road. I'm in a hurry. If I can't get by your car, I'll go through it! Savvy?'

She climbed back into the Range Rover and switched on the engine.

Lakenheath was tempted to accept the challenge, but the thought of the reaction of Mr Sayer, his explosive boss, to a wrecked car made him change his mind. Instead he put on his rueful, let's-patch-things-up grin and produced his key.

'All right,' he said. 'I'll move.'

She glowered back at him, but something in her education prevented her from being totally unresponsive to a truce flag.

'Please hurry,' she said. 'It's an emergency.'

Some phrases are nearly always counter-productive. Lakenheath paused in his progress to the Morris.

'Emergency,' he said in his clipped, emergency voice. 'Can I help?'

'Yes. You can move your bloody car! Oh, look. I'm sorry. But do hurry. I've lost somebody, my guardian, Dr Pasquino. He went off about midday and he hasn't come back yet and it's nearly five. I've been searching for him for the past couple of hours and now I think I ought to get a proper search going before dark. He might have slipped and broken something, or anything . . . !'

'Yes. Of course.' Lakenheath considered for a moment. 'Better get you to a telephone. The Old Kith Inn at Blackrigg, that's the nearest.'

'*That*,' she said with a restraint on her temper as obvious and uncertain as that exercised by her buttons on her breasts, 'is where I am heading. And *that* is where I would have been ten minutes ago if I hadn't had to waste my time talking to incompetent, ill-mannered and inconsiderate half-wits. *Move that bloody car!*'

She put the Range Rover into gear, Lakenheath leapt into the Morris and only a first time start and superb reverse acceleration got him out of her way in time.

'An impetuous young woman,' said Bulstrode, pushing Miss Amis into the back seat.

'Silly bitch,' said Lakenheath starting for the village. 'You can't help some people.'

As they approached the Old Kith, Bulstrode touched his arm and pointed at the Range Rover, abandoned with its door still open in front of the pub.

'Perhaps we should look in,' he said. 'Check that all's well. Besides, I could do with a drink.'

I daresay you could, thought Lakenheath bitterly. But can you do without it? The manner in which Bulstrode had disposed of five large gins, two bottles of claret and half a pint of brandy at lunch would have been impressive if the monthly argument with Sayer about the limits of his entertainment allowance had not taken place the day before.

'Surely,' he said, braking.

The first person they saw in the bar was the fat girl.

She had a large Scotch in front of her and a pensive look on her face.

' 'Evening, gents,' said the ancient leather-faced landlord from behind the bar. 'We're not really open, but what's it to be?'

Bulstrode ignored him.

'Everything under control, my dear?' he said to the girl.

'Yes thanks,' she said, made garrulous by relief, or by something, thought Lakenheath. 'At least I think so. There was a message waiting for me with Charley here. It seems that Leo, Dr Pasquino that is, did get a bit lost, but by chance he ran into someone who knew him, an old friend who's got a house up in Liddesdale somewhere. So he's gone there for dinner. And they rang Charley about an hour ago.'

'Well, that's extraordinary,' said Bulstrode. 'Just leaving you hanging around, worrying!'

'He's an extraordinary man,' said the girl defensively. 'Sometimes he doesn't think, that's all.'

'So your mad dash wasn't really necessary,' said Lakenheath smugly. 'Ah well. So it goes. Miss Amis, what will you drink?'

The girl turned her broad back on him and he steered Bulstrode and his secretary into the window-seat.

'You know, it is very pleasant here,' said Bulstrode, staring pensively through the leaded lights into the quiet street outside.

Lakenheath's keen ear thought it detected a sincere note in Bulstrode's voice. Could the man be weakening? If so, he ought to go into his spiel. That was what he was paid for.

'Isn't it?' he said. 'As you said yourself, Mr Bulstrode, the area is rich in potential. Take this village now. It'd be possible to retain most of it, the pub certainly, as the focal point of your company development. Obviously some of the cottages would have to give way before the new route

17

network, but the essential character of the place would be almost untouched and with modern landscaping techniques, factories can be tucked in anywhere. Look, let me show you what we had in mind. We had a projection done on the two-and-a-half-inch O.S. sheet, and you'll be amazed. I've got it in the car.'

He began to rise, then became aware that the plump girl was standing beside him.

'What's that you're saying?' she demanded. 'Knock down this village? Route networks? Factory sites? What the blazes is going on?'

'For heaven's sake!' said Lakenheath. 'Go and play somewhere else, there's a love. And do stop eavesdropping on adult conversations.'

'I'll eavesdrop as much as I like when I get a whiff of monstrous conspiracies like this!' she retorted. 'Who are you? What are you doing here?'

'I don't see how it's your business,' said Lakenheath, 'but I'm the chief officer of the North East Cumberland Development Council.'

'So that's it! Who'd have believed it? The dark satanic mills are trying to get their teeth in even up here. Wait till I tell Leo!'

She was flushed with anger once more. She really did turn an extraordinary colour when she was in a rage, thought Lakenheath. Like a Red Delicious apple.

'My job is to build up this part of the country,' he said coldly.

'Build up!' she interjected. 'By knocking down places where people have lived for centuries!'

She gestured dramatically at the street outside the window.

'Something needs to be done if people are going to go on living here for centuries,' Lakenheath answered 'God, I bet most of these houses were built out of wagon loads of stones hacked from poor old Hadrian's wall! And Johnnie Wade was happy enough to use half the wall

as foundations for his lovely road. None of your sentimental preservationists then!'

'What do you know about it, you pompous . . .'

She seemed stuck for a word extreme enough to capture
his demerits, or perhaps she knew the word but was
educationally inhibited from using it. Oily Bulstrode decided it was time to pour himself on troubled waters.

'Please,' he said. 'I think I started this. I was just
expressing my admiration for this charming village.'

He addressed himself to Lakenheath.

'You misunderstood me, I fear. My interest was a
purely personal one. I was just going to ask you if much
property came on the market up here? What a charming
holiday home two or three of these cottages would make
if they were run into one another. Outside would remain
quite unchanged, which would please our young friend
here, but what the eye doesn't see . . .'

He chuckled benevolently, feeling he had done his job
well.

The girl was staring at him incredulously. She had
passed the Red Delicious stage, Lakenheath noted, and
was not far short of the Red Cabbage.

'You're as bad as he is!' she finally exploded. 'Worse!
You want to come creeping in unannounced. At least
you can lie down in front of a bulldozer, but you can't
lie in front of dry rot! But you won't get away with it,
either of you. Forewarned is forearmed!'

She stormed angrily out of the bar and a moment later
the Range Rover's engine revved indignantly.

Lakenheath hoped she was going back up the moorland track to continue whatever odd activity had taken
her there in the first place. In her present mood she would
be lethal on the open road.

Bulstrode, showing his true Poly-fibre quality, was quite
unperturbed by the outburst. He had not ceased kneading
Miss Amis's leg under the table and now he pushed his
empty glass significantly towards Lakenheath.

'Well,' he said with a smile, 'at least we've taken her mind off her lost friend.'

This was true. But fifteen minutes later when Zeugma reached the site of her dig to tidy up and collect the implements her concern for Pasquino had made her leave strewn around, yet another loss had relegated Bulstrode and Lakenheath in their turn.

Incredulously she peered into the trench and wondered where on earth, or *anywhere*, an eighteen-hundred-year-old skeleton could have gone?

3

Afflictions induce callosities ; miseries are slippery or fall like snow upon us which notwithstanding is no unhappy stupidity.

'How long have you been on this job, Mr Lakenheath?'

'Six months, I think, Mr Sayer,' he answered, wondering if he should alter his Napoleonic pose by the wall map in his dusty little office. His interlocutor was sitting behind the large, old-fashioned desk whose top was impressively free of clutter. Lakenheath believed in a clutter-free desk. The minute Miss Peat in the outer office announced a visitor, he swept everything on the surface into a cardboard box which he then placed on top of the filing cabinet.

'So it was last September we appointed you.'

Lakenheath nodded and peered out of the window with an air of unconcern, looking down into the bustling little thoroughfare which was Front Street, Brampton. His office was at the top of a three-storied building and he had a good view of the little town. Friends had laughed when he had told them he would be centred on Brampton. One exiled native of the nearby metropolis of Carlisle had warned him, *they play tiggy with hammers there.* But Lakenheath liked it, liked the town, liked the people.

And his friend had been wrong. This sod at his desk wasn't using a hammer. He was using a pickaxe.

'September,' continued Sayer. 'Autumn. Middle of the financial year. No business would think of moving in autumn, you said. Then came the winter. You did some research on that, I recall. It's cold in winter, wasn't that what you found out? And now its spring. Things grow in spring, don't they? Or haven't you started your research yet?'

Sayer was a small man, but it was clear that inside that diminutive frame a very large and potentially destructive rage was trying to get out. N.E.C.D.C. was a project very dear to him for all kinds of reasons, but mainly because he had fallen out with the much larger and more stream-lined Cumberland Industrial Development Council over some detail of policy. N.E.C.D.C. was his attempt to cock a snook at the official body, and a very expensive snook it must be, thought Lakenheath guiltily.

Sayer moved to the wall map now and peered at it.

'What are these flags?'

'Red ones show our sites. Blue ones indicate potential customers.'

'Do they now? Let's see.'

He pulled one out and examined the lettering on it.

'Smithson Cans. They're out. Cherrilax. They're out. Hortifrolic? Who the hell are Hortifrolic?'

'They make garden gnomes. They're out.'

Another flag joined the growing pile on the floor.

'Which leaves two. Poly-fibre. That's that fellow Bulstrode, isn't it? Is he still around?'

'I think he'll be out at the golf club this morning. Checking on local amenities,' Lakenheath answered smartly.

The pin crumpled in Sayer's grip and the flag fluttered to the floor with the rest.

'Which leaves one. Charnell Bearings. What do they do?'

'If I had to hazard a guess, I'd say, make bearings.'

Sayer shot him a basilisk glance.

'Better than gnomes, I suppose. Let's have a look.'

'At what?'

'At what correspondence you've had with them, that's what. You have had correspondence with them?'

Lakenheath stepped smartly to the door, opened it and called, 'Miss Peat.'

After a full minute his secretary, who had to travel at least three yards, appeared. Lakenheath gazed at her in distaste. Poly-fibre gave you a Miss Amis, but the best North East Cumberland Development Council could run to was this. As her name suggested, she was brown and fibrous and capable of generating great heat.

'The Charnell Bearings file, Miss Peat,' commanded Lakenheath, crossing his fingers in his trouser pocket and hoping it wasn't in the cardboard box on top of the cabinet.

It wasn't. It occupied a drawer to itself in the filing cabinet and even Miss Peat's laboured movements could not make it look heavy.

Sayer opened the file and made a great show of examining its interior.

'Is this all?' he growled, drawing out a single sheet of paper.

'Yes.'

'*Dear Mr Lakenheath,*' Sayer read out loud. '*Many thanks for your literature which has roused a great deal of interest in our company. My congratulations to you on a very nicely organized and packaged presentation. If my directors share my enthusiasm, and I am sure they will, I hope to take advantage of your offer of an examination of potential sites. Of particular interest to us would be the former Research Centre on Thirlsike Waste but the whole area would be under consideration.*

Looking forward to an early meeting, yours sincerely, Mervyn Diss.'

'You've not replied?' demanded Sayer, shaking the empty file.

'I wrote personally. It seemed a useful contact, worth buttering up.'

'Did you? I suppose you smooth sods know how to treat your own. Well, Mr Lakenheath, it's precious little to show for six months' work, is it?'

'Things will liven up,' protested Lakenheath. 'The new presentation with the aerial photographs should rouse a lot of interest.'

'More damned expense! The only blasted interest you've roused so far was that gang of hippies who broke into the centre. Thank God we're shot of them. You can't take people round with scum like that cluttering up the place.'

'There were only four,' said Lakenheath.

'They're like the blacks,' said Sayer. 'Once they show up, they'll fill the place unless you act quick and get 'em out. Well, I shifted 'em, and I'll shift you too, my lad, if we don't get results soon!'

He made for the door, stopped and turned, almost catching Lakenheath's derisive gesture.

'And another thing. We're not an alcoholics' charity! Get that fellow Bulstrode off our slate before he drinks the county bankrupt!'

Now Sayer left, his efforts to slam the door thwarted by a warped frame. Lakenheath sat down at his desk and pondered. Sayer was an eminently dislikable man, but he had justice on his side. Payment by results would have left Lakenheath penniless, there was no denying it.

Instead of which, he thought solemnly, I am . . . penniless!

He whistled a dirge-like melody and crossed his legs on the desk. After a while he stopped whistling.

It was in this pose that Sergeant Fell found him.

'Excuse me, sir,' he said loudly.

Lakenheath woke and felt disconcerted by the man's presence. His relationship with the local police had not been untouched by discord and he had recently addressed himself to them in terms the recollection of which made him uneasy every time he parked his car.

'Good morning, Sergeant,' he said brightly. 'Can I help you?'

'I'm not sure, sir.' Fell looked at him assessingly. A big red-haired man with a bushy moustache, he had been very patient with Lakenheath, but the most placid mind can burn with resentment. However, now he looked worried rather than vengeful.

'Miss,' he said, 'is this the man?'

Lakenheath became aware of someone else in the room, or rather half in it. On the threshold with a look of sheepish obstinacy on her face was the fat girl who had attempted to run him over the previous day.

'Yes. That's him,' she said grimly.

Lakenheath swung his legs to the floor and sat upright in his chair.

Oh God! he thought incredulously. She's saying I've assaulted her!

'Sergeant,' he said. 'What's the trouble?'

Now Fell looked distinctly uneasy.

'Nothing really, sir. It's just that the young lady here, she says that . . . well, were you up on the common past Blackrigg yesterday, sir?'

'Yes, I was. What's this all about?'

'The thing is this, sir,' said Fell. 'The lady was doing what the archaeologists call a dig, and then she got a bit worried about her companion . . .'

'And she took off to look for him. Yes, yes, I know all that. Almost killing me *en route*. So?'

'When she returned to the site later, she found something was missing.'

'Missing? Oh, I see!' Lakenheath laughed, still incredulous but at the same time relieved. 'And she thinks Mr Bulstrode and I . . . how ridiculous!'

He laughed again. The girl began to flush that glowing fruity colour.

25

'All right,' he said. 'Tell me, what is it? What did you lose?'

The sergeant stepped back a pace as though dissociating himself from the proceedings.

'Well?' demanded Lakenheath.

'A skeleton,' snapped the girl.

'A skeleton!' echoed Lakenheath, and then began to laugh in earnest.

'They were old bones, she says,' said the sergeant, happy now the worst was over. 'Roman or something. Anyway, the young lady was at us all last evening about them, and she started again this morning. When we asked if she'd seen anyone else out that way yesterday, she suddenly mentioned you. Not by name, but what you were. For some reason, she seemed to think it was likely you might have picked up these bones, so here we are.'

As the sergeant spoke, Lakenheath became aware the girl was opening all the drawers in the filing cabinet and the stationery cupboard.

'What the hell are you doing?' he demanded.

'Look, miss, you've got no right . . .' began the sergeant.

'What's in that?' she interrupted. Her finger indicated the cardboard box on top of the cabinet.

'A body,' said Lakenheath. 'But it's not yours. It belongs to another little fat girl I strangled earlier.'

She reached up and pushed. The box slid away from her, teetered on the edge for a moment, then toppled, spreading across the floor an ashtray and its contents, copies of *The Times*, *Guardian*, *Mirror*, *Sun* and *Playboy*, a pack of cards, a doughnut with a bit out of it and an unopened bottle of Guinness.

'The doughnut may be Roman,' suggested Lakenheath.

'Oh, grow up!' snarled the girl, and left, succeeding with the door where Sayer had failed.

After he had recovered from the bang, the sergeant too prepared to depart.

26

'Sorry about all this, sir. You can't help us then? Very sorry, but she was most insistent.'

'I bet,' said Lakenheath. 'If you pursued legitimate investigations as thoroughly, you might get somewhere. Just leave the door.'

He stood and viewed the debris on the floor with distaste. The bottle of Guinness he picked up and locked in his desk. Then he went into the outer office where Miss Peat sat as unmoved by all the recent disturbance as an Easter Island statue by a heavy dewfall.

'I have to go out for a while,' said Lakenheath. 'If anyone calls, I'll be back after lunch. Oh, and tidy up my office a bit, there's a sweetie.'

He left, breathing in deeply as he stepped into the thin lemon-coloured spring sunshine, and walked briskly along Front Street to where his car was parked opposite the Conservative Club, one of Sayer's favourite haunts.

He had had enough of dwarf tyrants, vegetable secretaries and corpulent archaeologists. There were other things in life. He checked the golden hands of St Martin's clock in one direction against the white face of the Market House clock in the other and was pleased to see that the sacred and the profane for once agreed. By now Bulstrode should be puffing his way over the range of low fells on which the locals had masochistically sited their golf course. If the fine views over the Tarn did not hold him, there was a sufficiency of heather and gorse to delay his passage.

And Miss Amis? No one in his right mind would take Miss Amis on to a golf course. Not to play golf. She would doubtless still be at the Abbey Hotel near the village of Lanercost. The way to a businessman's heart could be through his secretary. Sayer might even count it as work.

With a last defiant glance toward the Conservative Club, he climbed into the old Morris and set off to earn his daily bread.

Zeugma, seated in a tiny café on the other side of the street, watched him go with distaste. Smug, smooth, self-centred, he was the blueprint of a hundred elder brothers who had paraded their pathetic charms round the school grounds on Open Days, each imagining that a mere feint of his hand towards his flies would send a dozen girls into anticipatory swoons. The only difference was that they at least were young.

Dismissing him from her mind (though recognizing glumly that once her anger faded, she would begin to feel guilty about that absurd scene in his office) she stirred her drinking chocolate and decided the time had come to 'look into herself'. The phrase was her old headmistress's, who advocated a bout of this interesting exercise at least once a day. Zeugma had let things slip during the last few years and sometimes herself went unlooked-into for months on end.

The school she attended had been Whitethorn in Sussex, where (according to the brochure) girls were prepared for both their traditional and their contemporary role in society. It catered mainly for the daughters of those whose military, political or business duties forced them to live abroad. Zeugma's father had been a minor but promising diplomat whose death by drowning in the Tigris while stationed in Baghdad had caused little stir. A keen natura-list, he had overreached in his efforts to trap some water-insect – or so went the theory.

As Zeugma's mother had vanished untraceably with a Peruvian civil servant during a short posting to Lima a few years previously, the family solicitor contacted the man designated in Arthur Gray's will as Zeugma's guard-ian. This was Leo Pasquino, F.S.A., Ph.D.

Pasquino was Arthur Gray's oldest friend. Of distant Italian extraction, he had contrived even at the age of thirty-five to establish himself in the main line of English

28

eccentrics. His eccentricity was partly a pose in order to facilitate extraction from patrons and public of the monies necessary to his many archaeological projects. But pose quickly becomes posture and though feathers may be fluttered and fluffed, they are none the less part of the bird.

Arriving at Whitethorn to examine the new charge which fate had placed on his account, he had critically examined the podgy thirteen-year-old who stood before him, then asked the headmistress, 'Is she finished yet?'

'Finished?' replied Miss Akenside. 'She cannot yet be said properly to have begun.'

Thereafter Pasquino treated the school as a kind of oven into which he peered from time to time to see if Zeugma were done. It was a slow process and spotted with moments of despair. At thirteen, half of her coevals were as fat as she was. Two years later, the proportions were significantly changed, and at the age of seventeen Zeugma was convinced she was the fattest girl in the world. Even her friends called her Humpty, a habit Pasquino had picked up (and still, distressingly, retained).

At eighteen Pasquino had decided that she was as *done* as she was ever likely to get at Whitethorn and offered her a straight choice. University for three years to carry her through to the age of majority and self-govern-ment (still twenty-one in 1968), or she could join him as a kind of baggage-master-labourer-amanuensis.

She thought for only a minute and chose. The bits of holiday she had spent with Pasquino had given her a genuine interest in archaeology, but it wasn't just this that swayed her. She had had enough of being educated, and the company of her slim fellow pupils was beginning to pall. The thought of three years as a fat undergraduate was vile.

Thus began five years of travel, trial and tribulation, hard work and constant learning. Pasquino was an archaeological gadfly, dismissed as flighty and unsound by some of the more conservative elements in the business, but with a disconcerting habit of turning visible theory into incontrovertible fact. His siting of the Roman light-house at Deal had proved accurate within ten metres (*their fault, not mine,* he said); his interpretations of Linear A, though not generally accepted, caused great scholarly interest; and his theory that American Indians may have discovered Norway shot him into the ken of the general public. He was not invariably right, but often enough, and the newspapers loved him. He had fought in Korea where he lost an eye through his discovery of what he thought might be a Macedonian sherd when digging a slit trench and his subsequent slowness to take cover when the shells started falling.

Zeugma had soon begun to realize that a great deal of hard work and careful investigation usually preceded a Pasquino intuitive flash. There was always a starting point, more often than not the acceptably scholarly one of a learned article reporting a bit of recent field work. But sometimes a snippet of folklore, a local tradition or, as in the present case, an accidental glimpse of some aerial photographs was enough to set him off.

And once he was off, there was no knowing where he would stop.

At present it was where he had stopped the previous night that was bothering Zeugma. Not that she was concerned about his well-being – such erratic behaviour fell well within his concept of the permissible – but she was concerned about his reaction to her own activities. She hadn't really set out to make a fuss about the bones; it had been an accumulative thing, provoked by the amuse-ment or disbelief of those she had mentioned the loss to. Not to be taken seriously was a cross she had long ago decided to drop by the roadside, but it required almost as much effort to do this as to lug it to the top of the hill. Normally Pasquino would applaud her efforts, but not if they drew unwanted attention to his current activities. Zeugma was uneasily aware of the interesting little newspaper story this would make.

She ran through a mental check-list. The police would be discreet, avoiding like the plague anything which might bring her into their midst once more. Old Charley at Blackrigg and his customers would no more think of contacting the local press than they would of revealing their incomes to the Inland Revenue.

Which left only one. The polluter, the dark, satanic mills man. Lakenheath. Even the name rang sinisterly.

He had been considerably provoked, she had to admit. If he wanted to take his revenge by making her look foolish in that little *comic-cuts* section at the foot of page one in the *Guardian*, it would be understandable.

She was still a long way from the guilt feeling she knew she would eventually reach, but this new motive of self-interest weighed strong.

Lakenheath would have to be placated. And quickly.

Two minutes later she descended the stairs from the N.E.C.D.C. office, having extracted from a grudging Miss Peat the information that her employer was out, which she knew, and would return, which she guessed. She decided to go to the police station and soothe the frayed nerves there.

As she left the building, a large black Buick slid silently into the two English parking spots next to the Range Rover.

Out of it stepped a dark-suited man, his hair trimmed unfashionably short, like an astronaut's. He was young, but there was a stillness about him which made you forget his youth. He stood by the car and watched Zeugma cross the street. His face had that menacing blankness with which the film-makers have so ingeniously overcome the language problem in spaghetti westerns.

Zeugma felt challenged. It was a psychological hazard with her. She filled the known world with imagined challenges to her right to exist. And she answered as many of them as she could.

Now she stood by the Range Rover and returned the stranger's stare. He it was that moved first and disappeared through the door which led to Lakenheath's office.

But as Zeugma drove away she felt far from victorious.

4

*Many of these Urnes were broke by a
vulgar discoverer in hope of enclosed
treasure . . . Where profit hath prompted,
no age hath wanted such miners.*

Lakenheath discovered Miss Amis looking very bored in
the chintzy lounge of the Abbey Hotel. Things started
well and she agreed without demur when he proposed a
short drive.

It was very short indeed. After less than a minute he
pulled off the road beside the ruins of Lanercost Priory
after which the hotel was mis-named.

'Have you seen the priory?' he asked.

'No', she said.

He took this to mean that she had not walked round
the remains, though it might well mean she just had not
noticed their existence.

'Come on,' he said, 'It's very interesting.'

They walked beneath the ruined arch and past the
gatehouse in which Edward the First had been received
by the monks, information which Miss Amis received
with considerable indifference. Undaunted, he put his
arm round her waist and suggested they rested on the
parapet of the cloister wall to drink in atmosphere. She
twisted expertly out of his grip and replied that she felt
gin would do her more good.

Personally trained by Bulstrode, thought Lakenheath

33

gloomily as she strolled away from him. He thrust his hands deep into the pockets of his sheepskin jacket and returned her gaze sourly as she turned to see if he was following her.

Then her glance moved upwards, her eyes and mouth rounded to circles, like a facial pawnbroker's sign, and she said, 'Oh!'

As a warning it was little enough, but it made Lakenheath glance upwards in time to see the large block of sandstone tumbling lazily down on him. He jumped to one side, slipped on the damp grass and fell awkwardly, twisting his ankle beneath him. The stone struck the ground less than a yard away, showering him with lumps of earth.

'Are you all right?' said Miss Amis.

He didn't answer but rose slowly, wincing as he put his weight on his injured ankle. It wasn't badly hurt, merely slightly twisted, but the pain was enough to put him in mind of the effects of receiving half a hundredweight of twelfth-century sandstone on his head.

It wasn't his lucky season, he decided ruefully. There had been other incidents recently. He'd had a blow-out in the Morris the previous week and a few days before that he'd almost been knocked down by a motor-bike. And there seemed little chance of a compensatory improvement to his sexual fortunes.

Satisfied he was able to move, Miss Amis had resumed her progress towards the car. Glumly he brushed down his jacket and followed.

There was another vehicle parked next to his now, a Range Rover. He looked round suspiciously. There, sure enough, standing over by the farm which adjoined the priory ruins was the fat girl. She must have seen, and doubtless enjoyed, his discomfiture. Now she was walking towards him. Quickly he got into the Morris, started the engine and drove away from the priory. In the mirror he saw the Range Rover start up too. Miss Amis seemed

34

to have gone to sleep in the passenger seat.

No wonder men became monks.

Zeugma kept her distance behind the Morris. It had been mere coincidence that she had come across Lakenheath at the ruins. It seemed an unlikely place to find him, though the presence of that spindly secretarial camp-follower indicated his real motives. Her opinion of the man had been confirmed by her recent discussion with Sergeant Fell, who had become almost garrulous when he realized she had come to close the matter of the bones. Lakenheath, he had replied to her queries, was a good man to pacify. He seemed to like stirring up trouble as in the matter of the hippies in the old research centre. Zeugma would have got the full blow-by-blow story if she had cared to press, but foreseeing that her own feelings about the centre plus her views on the rights of minorities would displease Fell even more than the fascist extremism of the N.E.C.D.C. line, she had left while all was still sweetness and light.

She had come to the priory ruins to meditate, had spotted Lakenheath, decided this was not a good time to approach him with feelings of such bitter dislike in her heart, then, as though in response to some angry impulse of her own, the stone had fallen. She had opened her mouth to cry out, but not been able to.

Now she followed, her anger against the man dulled by a stronger sense of unease at what she had just witnessed. Or perhaps 'witnessed' was too strong.

But it had seemed for a moment as the stone fell that a shadow had moved behind the parapet from which it had been dislodged. And though her further examination had produced no evidence that anyone else was in the ruins at that time, her sense of a presence was too strong for her to wish to remain any longer after Lakenheath's departure.

She arrived back in Brampton just in time to see Lakenheath limping through the door of the building which housed his office. He must have shoved the girl out at the hotel almost without stopping, she thought, as she parked the Range Rover and prepared to get her own distasteful task of conciliation over.

Though Zeugma took her time in crossing the road, Lakenheath's even slower progress had just got him to the top of the stairs. He turned, attracted by the sound of the opening door, shuddered at the sight of her and shouted with more anger than the occasion seemed to demand, 'What the hell do you want?'

'Just a word,' she said, starting to ascend. She affected nonchalance, but to climb those steep narrow stairs to the angry man who stood half in shadow at the top required a positive act of will. For a moment she thought he was just going to stand there blocking her way but then he shook his head and said in a voice more pleading than wrathful, 'Look, I haven't got your sodding bones.'

He turned and went into his office before she could reply. She followed him. Miss Peat looked up from her typewriter and opened her mouth as if to speak, but even Lakenheath's limp did not slow him down sufficiently for the words to emerge before he reached his own office door.

He pushed it open and stopped abruptly. Zeugma almost ran into him, and round his shoulders she saw what had caused the halt. Sitting behind Lakenheath's desk was the man from the Buick.

'Hello,' said Lakenheath neutrally. 'Who're you?'

He was irritated, Zeugma sensed, but not so irritated that he would run the risk of offending someone who might be important. No, he would vent his irritation on troublesome females of whose unimportance he was quite convinced. I come in peace, Zeugma reminded herself anxiously. I mustn't let him provoke me.

The Buick man slowly rose, walked round the desk

with the measured tread of a cat minding its own business, and held out his hand.

'Mr Lakenheath?' he said in a flat American accent. 'I'm Mervyn Diss.'

Lakenheath took the hand in a gesture which from behind looked more reflex than welcoming.

'Diss?' he repeated.

'That's right. Diss. Charnell Bearings.'

His gaze slipped round Lakenheath and fastened upon Zeugma. At this range it was even harder to bear than it had been in the street and she stepped back half a pace.

Lakenheath turned now and looked at her as if he had never seen her before in his life.

'Mr Lakenheath,' said Zeugma in her best headmistress-creep voice, 'I wanted to say how sorry . . .'

'Please,' said Lakenheath very gently. 'Not now.'

He looked back at Diss as if suspecting that he might have been an apparition, vanishing as suddenly as he had appeared.

'Yes, well, I just hope that . . .' Zeugma began again.

'For Christ's sake! I said not now! Can't you see I'm busy? Just push off, will you?'

This was more like it. This was the authentic male chauvinist polluter in full cry. Zeugma forgot her vows of humility.

'Yes, I can see you're busy!' she said. 'Busy planning to tear up a bit more of the countryside in the name of progress. But you try it, just you go and try it and I'll, I'll . . .'

Zeugma, shaking with rage, found herself like King Lear unable to complete her threat though knowing it would be the terror of the earth. Also she found herself being expertly shepherded out of the door on to the landing. Like a good sheepdog, Lakenheath never actually touched his stray ewe, but kept her moving by a series of short economical feints. She decided to make a last stand at the top of the stairs, but a slight though infinitely

37

menacing movement of his head caused her to step back once more. Her foot found nothing to step on to and she realized she had reached the stairs themselves when Lakenheath's expression changed from purposeful wrath to wrathful anxiety. He grabbed at her, she grabbed at him; for a moment a stasis seemed to have been achieved; then together they collapsed sideways against the wall and slid slowly down the first half-dozen stairs.

Zeugma was the first to recover. She was relieved to find she was unharmed except for a couple of bruises and she looked down at the still recumbent Lakenheath, uncertain whether to thank him or kick him.

'Are you all right?' he asked. He looked rather pale himself and she decided that perhaps she had better not be too hard on him.

'Yes thanks,' she said.

'I'm sorry,' he said. 'I underestimated your weight.'

That did it. She swung back her foot, aiming at a point just above the ankle which memories of Whitethorn hockey field assured her was particularly vulnerable. Then she became aware of witnesses. Above, Diss watched impassively, while below a new figure, a middle-aged rather short man, gazed in amazement at the violent tableau.

'Here,' he called. 'What's going on? Stop that, Lakenheath!'

The short man ascended. Zeugma looked at him approvingly. Clearly he was ready to believe that the scene was all organized by Lakenheath for some perverse pleasure. Such things, her well-travelled friends at Whitethorn had assured her, were commonplace in Hamburg, Port Said and South Kensington.

'Oh, hello, Mr Sayer,' said Lakenheath, trying to rise.

'Ohh!' he groaned and subsided.

'What's the trouble?' said Sayer suspiciously.

'My ankle. I turned it earlier and now it's really gone.'

Zeugma bent down and pulled back his sock. The ankle

was swelling almost visibly, as though glad to be free of the restricting wool. It was, she realized, the very ankle into which she had been about to bury the reinforced toe-cap of her walking boot.

They helped him stumblingly to the top of the stairs, where Diss reached forward and, with an ease which mocked their efforts, picked Lakenheath bodily from their hands and set him down in the office.

'Chair,' he said to Miss Peat, who, to everyone's amazement, moved at great speed to set one behind Lakenheath, who sank into it gratefully.

During the next few minutes, Zeugma was surprised to notice she herself was the only one who displayed any kind of solicitude about the injured ankle, including Lakenheath himself. The man Diss introduced himself to Sayer, who seemed very impressed and proportionately apologetic about the embarrassment of the scene which had just taken place. Lakenheath kept on trying to join the conversation, verbally and physically, but every time he tried to stand up with a view to hopping towards the other two, Zeugma, who was removing his shoe, jabbed her forefinger into the swelling and he subsided with a groan.

Miss Peat just sat, hands poised over her keyboard.

'I was hoping to do a site tour first thing tomorrow morning,' Diss was saying. 'To ensure we are not wasting our time.'

'You won't be, you won't be,' said Sayer, shaking his head emphatically. 'Mr Lakenheath, our chief officer . . .'

He turned and looked at Mr Lakenheath, his chief officer, observed with horror the size of the swelling, and continued with some irritation, 'Mr Lakenheath clearly won't be able to take you, so . . .'

'Yes, I will. Yes, I will,' protested Lakenheath, surprising Zeugma, who had not read him as the show-must-go-on-type. 'Of course I will. Just hold on a mo.'

They watched in silence as he vainly attempted to replace his sock, which Zeugma was interested to note had a large darn in the toe. It was no contest.

'. . . so I shall take you myself,' continued Sayer. 'Have you come straight here? Yes. Then Miss Peat will book you a room at the Abbey Hotel. It's *en route*, so I'll call for you at nine, shall I? Miss Peat, get on to the Abbey, will you?'

Diss walked past Zeugma and Lakenheath without a glance in their direction. Sayer was close behind, as though fearful of losing contact.

'I'm all right,' insisted Lakenheath as he passed. 'I could take him.'

But he didn't sound as if he believed it himself.

'Don't be a fool,' said Sayer coldly. 'Miss Peat, ring for a doctor. If I were you, Lakenheath, I'd concentrate on getting on your feet again as quickly as possible.'

He left and they heard him pattering down the stairs to make up the ground he had lost on Diss.

'Damn, damn, damn, damn, damn,' said Lakenheath. 'Oh damn!'

He stood up, tried to move towards his own office, stumbled after only a couple of hops and came to rest on Zeugma's shoulder. She helped him through the door with more vigour than gentleness and deposited him in the chair just vacated by Diss.

'Thanks,' he said. He leaned forward and pulled open a drawer, taking from it a Guinness bottle which she recognized from her first visit. He banged off the cap on the side of his desk and caught the resultant gush of foam and liquid in his mouth without losing a drop. When he put the bottle down it was almost empty.

'Medicinal,' he said. 'Now if we could get *them* to come up here . . .'

He sighed and finished the bottle.

'Why do you want *anyone* to come up here?'

'Why not? All that land lying there doing nothing, it's a waste.'

'Don't be so stupid! It's not doing nothing,' protested Zeugma. 'Things grow on it, and animals and birds and insects exist because of it. Sheep graze on it, and some people even depend on it for a living!'

'I note you always leave people to the last,' he said scornfully. 'Your kind always do.'

'My kind!' she screeched in anger. 'It's not *my kind* who go about persecuting harmless minority groups who prefer to opt out of your concrete-and-glass society.'

'Meaning?'

'Meaning those people who squatted in the Thirlsike Centre, that's who.'

'Oh. So you heard about them,' he said quietly.

'Yes, I heard. It must be the first useful purpose that blasted eyesore has served. And you chucked them out. In the middle of winter too. Did you ever think what became of them, Mr Lakenheath?'

He looked at her with such dislike that she stepped back as though he had offered to strike her. Then his expression relaxed.

'The centre *was* built for a purpose,' he said. 'That purpose over, it's part of my job to find another purpose for it. It harmed no one. It was built in the middle of a waste – Thirlsike Waste, I didn't invent the name – it disturbed no one . . .'

'What? Not disturbed? Do you know when they were ploughing up the ground for the foundations they came upon a Bronze Age urn-field? *That* the local archaeologists found out about, but too late to do anything but preserve a few urns. God knows what else was just bulldozed under! I believe in people, Mr Lakenheath, but people in the past, the present *and* the future!'

She realized she was shouting and took a deep breath.

'But I haven't come here to quarrel with you, Mr Lakenheath,' she resumed quietly. 'I came to apologize for what happened this morning, that's all. I'm sorry, and I hope that the matter can be allowed to rest there.

Now I'll leave you. The doctor should be here shortly.'

'You don't want any fuss!' observed Lakenheath suddenly before she could leave. 'That's it! You don't want to look silly on Border Television! Girl archaeologist loses ancient companion and even more ancient bones!'

Zeugma felt her cheeks flush darkly at the accuracy of this nauseating man's guess. He took this for the admission it was and laughed openly for a moment, then stopped abruptly.

'All right,' he said. 'I'll accept your apology. In return perhaps you might care to do me a little favour.'

'What?' she said suspiciously.

'Nothing really. This ankle, it's going to be a nuisance. No driving, I should think, for a while. Now, my job takes me all over the area, particularly up on the waste. You act as my chauffeur tomorrow in that expensive van of yours, and I'll forget I ever heard of the incredible vanishing bones. How's that?'

'It's blackmail!' she answered indignantly, feeling the impulse stronger than ever to launch a total physical attack on the inane complacency of the face before her.

'It's a favour,' he insisted. 'That's all. Okay? Good. Nine-thirty in the morning then.'

'Go to hell,' she said.

'It's up to you,' he said indifferently.

Zeugma paused at the door.

'I hope you get gangrene,' she said distinctly. 'It shouldn't be difficult for someone in your dirty business.'

The noise she made as she slammed the door was music to her ears. Miss Peat did not even look up.

5

Time hath endless rarities and shows of all varieties.

The bloody girl's not going to turn up, thought Lakenheath gloomily.

It was quarter to ten and for the last twenty minutes he had been attracting the amused but non-malicious attention of passers-by. The inmates of a small country town have to make their own entertainment and they rapidly seize the opportunities offered by a man seated on a shooting stick wedged in a crack in the pavement, particularly when his left foot is covered by a wellington boot and his right by a Turkish-style carpet slipper.

It would have been better to wait inside, he thought, but he had omitted to tell the stupid woman that he lived in the hotel at the other side of the town square, and it seemed foolish to climb those fatal stairs merely to descend them again a few moments later.

The weather was changing. The sun still shone, but a stiff wind was blowing ragged banners of cloud across the sky, producing a curiously artificial effect, like a badly projected cyclorama. Occasional gusts were strong enough to threaten his overthrow, an event eagerly anticipated by a group of women who had booked the grandstand window seat in the little café opposite.

I'll give her another five minutes, he thought. The temptation to say *to hell with it* ! and spend a day baiting traps for a not-unattractive Scottish chambermaid, who

43

from time to time bared her teeth at him in a kind of threatening invitation, was strong. But the pull of self-interest is stronger and the thought of Sayer shepherding Diss around the area all day filled him with such unease that he had foolishly put his trust in the little fat girl with the Range Rover. Perhaps he shouldn't have tried to blackmail her. She looked the type who might have responded more readily to some form of sentimentalism. A soft touch. Christ yes, she looked *that* all right. As if she was padded with Dunlopillo!

The thought made him smile broadly.

'I'm glad to see you looking so happy,' said Zeugma.

'You're here! Where the hell have you been?'

She didn't answer but engaged gear as he slid into the passenger seat.

He waved at the openly disappointed café women as they moved away.

'They're going to miss me,' he said with some complacency.

'How's your ankle?' she asked.

'A slight sprain,' he said dismissively. 'You needn't feel guilty.'

Zeugma felt herself getting angry again.

'Oh, ball-bearings!' she snapped. This fairly innocent explosion reduced Lakenheath to a surprising almost introspective quietness for a while.

The silence lasted till the gentle but steady incline of the road had taken them out of the familiar agricultural countryside which lay around Brampton up into the fringes of the high bleak moorlands which run away to Scotland in the north and east. Lakenheath spoke in the end out of a desire to interrupt his own thoughts rather than a need for small-talk.

'Has whatsit come back yet?' he asked. 'Your absent professor. Pagliacci.'

'Dr Pasquino,' she corrected. 'No. He's still staying in Liddesdale.'

Something in her voice caught his attention away from his own troubles.

'You've spoken to him?' he asked casually.

'No. Not exactly. Well, that's it,' she said with no kind of precision. He didn't say anything. If there was more to come, it would come without prompting.

'When I got back to the Old Kith yesterday afternoon, I thought he'd probably be back. Instead someone had been and collected his stuff. A young man, Charley said.'

'But was there no message?' asked Lakenheath, puzzled.

'Oh yes.'

She reached into the breast pocket of her bright red shirt and with difficulty eased a piece of paper out.

Lakenheath took it. The calligraphy was elegantly indecipherable, a seventeenth-century hand. It took him some moments to interpret the message.

Sorry to have missed you, it read. *Leo is stopping for a couple of days and needs a change of socks! He sends his love and hopes you are making good progress with the work. He'll ring you at the pub tonight or tomorrow.*

It was signed *Jonathan Upas.*

'Who's he?' asked Lakenheath. 'The name rings a bell.'

'It's quite well known in the Borders evidently,' said Zeugma. 'I asked Charley. He hadn't recognized the young man but the minute I mentioned the name he was able to give forth. It seems there was a Colonel Upas of Liddesdale who was a kind of low-key Glubb Pasha with a touch of the Lawrences in some Middle East oil state. He went up in smoke during a coup in the early fifties, thus saving his masters the trouble of paying his plane fare home when they sacked him. This was pretty certain it seems, despite the fact that he had almost gone native, embracing Islam and marrying a local lass. There were three children, two boys and a girl. They inherited his Scottish property of course and from time to time they spend a few weeks here. They keep very much to themselves, but even total invisibility wouldn't keep a stranger totally out of Charley's ken!'

'Yes, I thought I knew the name,' said Lakenheath slowly. 'Well, at least that explains how your guardian knew them. I suppose he's done a lot of jaunting around in North Africa. What did he say when he rang?'

'Well, he didn't you see,' she answered. 'I tried to ring him but the exchange said the Upas's number was ex-directory and the stupid fools wouldn't let me have it.'

She spoke so angrily that Lakenheath laughed.

'They're not horses, you know,' he said. 'You can't always get your own way by shouting. Relax. Enjoy yourself.'

'Oh, let it drop,' Zeugma snapped angrily. 'It's my concern and can't possibly be of any interest to you.'

'Now she tells me,' said Lakenheath, then with a broad grin added unexpectedly, 'Though of course it *is* my concern too, in a way. It suddenly strikes me, that's why I'm here! If you'd got their number and rung it, and talked to dear Leo, that would have been the end of it! Off you'd have gone to your precious hole happy as a sandboy and I'd have still been printing a pretty pattern on my buttocks in the middle of Brampton. But dear Leo isn't there to advise you, you're a bit uncertain, a bit bothered, so much so that you begin to think you might as well pick up nasty old Lakenheath after all. Any company's better than none, and besides, he's such a prick, he could still spread that comic tale about the bones around!'

It was (for the second time in twenty-four hours) such an accurate analysis of her private thoughts and motives that Zeugma felt herself turning puce with fury. She concentrated her mind with fierce intensity on the nastiest thing in the world. This was having your eyes put out prior to being raped, a suggestion which a Whitethorn confidante had assured her was actually contained in the

Turkish Officers' Training Manual up to the signing of the Geneva Convention. *It's easier if they can't see*, her friend had averred confidently, enjoying the horror within the confines of her limited empathy. It had made Zeugma quite ill. Not the notion of rape, though that was unpleasant enough, but the thought of losing her eyes. She had once seen Leo slipping his glass eye into place and had almost fainted. But being a practical girl, she had endeavoured to turn a weakness into a strength and the blood-draining properties of this particular thought had come in very handy when she felt herself over-reddening through anger or embarrassment.

After a while she felt able to speak again.

'Where would you like to go?' she asked equably.

Lakenheath had been too immersed in his own thoughts to pay much attention to Zeugma's inner struggles. In any case he now accepted speechless rage as her most common mental state.

'Oh, just drive around a bit,' he said vaguely.

'Look, I do have things of my own to do,' protested Zeugma.

'All right then. Make for the Thirlsike Research Centre. This thing will go over the waste, won't it?'

'Why, yes. But there's a perfectly good road. In fact, typically, as it was built to be used by lorries and security men and civil servants instead of the people who actually live round here, it's the best road in the area.'

'I wouldn't want you to be compromised by actually using it,' said Lakenheath gravely.

Zeugma pondered her companion's real reasons for not wishing to use the road as a little further on she switched into four-wheel drive and sent the Range Rover clambering up the moorland slopes with which she was now very familiar.

He must, she deduced, be expecting to find Sayer and Diss at the centre already and for some reason he did not want them to see him making a frontal approach.

But why he should wish to spy on his boss and his client, she could not begin to imagine.

Her theory was confirmed when twenty minutes later they reached the crest of a ridge overlooking the centre.

'Hold it,' said Lakenheath. 'Run back down the slope a bit, will you?'

She acquiesced without comment, reversing till the ridge lay between themselves and the centre.

'Your boss is here then,' she said as she applied the brakes.

'He's not my boss,' replied Lakenheath. But he too had seen the distinctive shape of the ancient Morris parked just inside the gates. He had noticed that the car had gone from its usual parking spot that morning. Trust Sayer to be too mean to use his own three-and-a-half-litre Rover on official business!

'He talks to you as if he were,' said Zeugma.

'You talk to me as if I were Attila the Hun and you the Virgin Mary.'

Lakenheath scrambled uneasily from the car and limped to the crest of the ridge where he leaned forward on his shooting stick, looking for a moment like a hill farmer watching his dog rounding up his scattered sheep.

'Why do you let him push you around then?'

'He's got some importance in the set-up that hired me. And he enjoys doing a lot of his own barking.'

'While you feel it should be you, the professional polluter, down there selling that mess?'

'Something like that,' said Lakenheath. His attention was too firmly concentrated on *that mess* to react to this gibe.

The Thirlsike Centre had been built in the early sixties as part of the European attempt to establish a rocket technology not too far behind the Russian and American. There were other centres for related research projects, like the one at nearby Spadeadam, but Thirlsike was the one which concentrated on purely military matters, namely

48

the development of a new fuel for Bucephalus, the great European anti-anti-missile missile, bits of which now littered the deserts of Australia to the fury of prospectors equipped with geiger-counters.

The centre had been built in this remote area partly for security reasons and partly because even government planners could see that an establishment capable, at a rough estimate, of producing a hole half a mile wide should some disaster occur was not best suited for an urban site.

Thirlsike Waste had had a similar attraction to early nineteenth-century planners for different reasons. Then an old farmhouse, uninhabited since its owners had been snowed up in the fierce winter of 1798 and died of cold and starvation, had been converted into a fever hospital to cope with an epidemic of typhoid which had ravaged the north half of Cumberland. The track to the farmhouse had been hastily improved with cartloads of loose stone and this same track had been the basis of the present modern road which Lakenheath could see running vacantly away to the south.

The fever hospital had been in use only a few years, but the centre builders in one of those absurd (and usually expensive) fits of 'economy' so beloved by government departments had used the old building, or what remained of it, as the centrepiece of the centre. Around it ran the quadrangle of laboratories, test chambers and offices where the great work had been carried out until amid an increasing volume of protest both internal and external the project had been wound down, closing completely six months earlier. In a way Lakenheath suspected that the centre's closure had helped create his own job. Here was not only a site, but plant with a good access road. Surely somebody must want it?

But so far nobody had. It was a dismal, depressing-looking place and Lakenheath could not blame prospective customers for sheering off when they saw it. The waste had already sent in its pioneer forces of frost, wind and seed to commence the task they had been performing on the Romans for the past fifteen centuries. The story of the manner in which the last owners of the old farm had died was still told locally as if it had been just last year, and the same locals had nodded knowingly when within a month of his leaving the centre, the local paper reported that Dr Arthur Healot, the former research director, had been found hanging from a skylight in a California motel.

Zeugma interrupted these cheerful thoughts with the not unreasonable demand, 'What now?'

He looked at her thoughtfully. Out here under the open sky with a fresh wind blowing and the earth burgeoning with new life, she looked rather different. In place, as it were. Healthy, vital, belonging.

'Look, I don't want to keep you from your work,' he said, 'so if you could leave me here and collect me in, say, a couple of hours, that'd give you a chance to get on with whatever it is you're doing.'

His solicitude for her archaeological project was manifestly so spurious that it couldn't even be called hypocritical.

'If that's what you want,' she said.

Two minutes later he was seated in his chosen place with a car rug round his shoulders to ward off the now biting wind and his binocular case in his hand.

'What are you going to do?' she asked.

'I like watching birds,' he said. 'See you later.'

I hope it rains, thought Zeugma maliciously as she drove away. I hope it pees down.

But the clouds at present were being whipped far too rapidly across the sky to have much time to shed their loads and she was concentrating too hard on her driving to bear malice for long. The terrain up here was exceptionally treacherous and Leo would not be pleased if she

50

got the Range Rover stuck or, worse still, damaged it. At least there was no other traffic to bother about, and precious few pedestrians.

As though conjured up by her thought, one of the latter now appeared. He was about two hundred yards off and below her and being chased by a wolf. No, she corrected herself as the running order changed, he was chasing a wolf. Fascinated by this sight, she let the front nearside wheel sink into one of the soft patches and only a rapid bit of gear manoeuvring kept her out of trouble. With her full attention returned to driving, she only caught occasional glimpses of the strange pursuit (if such it was) going on ahead.

She finally overtook them on a line about fifty feet to their left and risked a sideways glance. The wolf was not, she deduced, really a wolf but the nearest thing you could get to it this side of the Steppes. It was as though someone had started with a pair of Alsatians and gradually bred out the refinements.

There was something lupine about the man also. Head thrust forward and held low, large yellow teeth bared with the effort of running, a wildness round the eyes deep sunk in a weather beaten leathery face, he could have been almost any age. He was clad in what looked like a pair of cream-coloured tights with cross-over braces, a costume she recalled seeing Cumberland wrestlers wear at some of the local games.

Then the ground fell away steeply but more smoothly in front of her and she was able to let the Range Rover surge away from the strange pair, neither of whom had shown the least awareness of her presence.

The site of the dig was a quarter of a mile further on, in the trough of a shallow basin. Zeugma aproached it with an unenthusiasm that troubled her for all sorts of reasons. Lakenheath had been right. Being out of touch with Leo like this had upset the whole balance of her being. She had not been able to finish the three eggs and half pound of bacon which Charley set as a matter of course before those privileged to be his guests. But loss of appetite was only a symptom. More important was the loss of that feeling of self-sufficiency which had been one of the compensations for five years spent moving at speeds too great for the setting down of roots. Of course she had met a lot of people, some pretty important, that was inevitable when you worked with Leo. And there had been men as well. Two anyway.

The latest had been the 'Keats' autumn episode with a medieval history student helping with the dig at Cadbury, a relationship broken off by Pasquino's intuitive decision that there was nothing more to find there and the quest for Arthur must be pursued to the north. She sometimes flattered herself with the thought that perhaps it was Leo's desire to keep her away from the student as much as Arthur's erratic movements which had caused the change of plan. But Leo had not said or done anything to confirm this hypothesis.

He hadn't approved (she suspected) of her earlier and much more serious affair either. It was five years ago now, she realized. Five years since she had met, loved, gone to bed with, and, without explanation or farewell, been abandoned by Hasan bin Radhauri. It was through Leo that she had met Hasan in Cairo. Suave, urbane, highly educated, about ten years older than herself, he had seemed an unlikely candidate for the favours of a plump, rather awkward and freely perspiring English girl. Yet it had happened and had continued to happen for five short weeks which now had the flimsy quality of a pleasurable dream.

Then he had gone and a few days later Leo had had another of his famous intuitions and whisked her off to southern Ireland. The next few years had been busy ones, too busy for anything more than an occasional grapple with a superannuated academic at some archaeological conference. Even the medieval history student affair had not really touched her. She was, she had begun to think, completely self-sufficient. And now just because of Leo's perfectly in-character disappearance for a couple of days, she was feeling like Marianna in the Moated Grange and even taking up with shits like Lakenheath just for the sake of company!

A day's good hard work should get this nonsense out of my system, she told herself angrily, and sent the Range Rover bouncing over the lip of the basin where the dig was located.

Someone was there already.

Leo, she thought for a moment. But only for a moment. Leo was longer, thinner, older than the figure who watched her approach now. Nor did Leo ride a motor-bike and wear black leather. So it wasn't Leo. But who it was remained quite impossible to deduce even when she drew up alongside the bike as the top half of his face was covered by a huge pair of dust-caked goggles and his chin rested in a casually knotted white silk scarf.

She stared at him silently out of the car window, feeling irrationally that if she spoke first he might pull back the goggles and the scarf to reveal the skull which had disappeared two days before from the canvas-covered trench behind him.

'Hello,' she said abruptly. 'Can I help you?'

He pushed back the goggles and peeled off the leather balaclava which had made his head look like a large black egg. He was young, dark complexioned (which showed off his even white teeth as he smiled at her) and had the unusual combination of jet-black hair and light-blue eyes. He was also very good looking and she fought hard to resist taking an instant liking to him. Distrust first impressions, she had been taught at Whitethorn.

'Zeugma Gray?' he said. 'If you're Zeugma Gray, I've been assured you will provide me with coffee, one of Charley's pork and crackling sandwiches, and intellectual conversation.'

'Assured who by?'

'By Leo, of course. I'm Jonathan Upas.'

He held out a hand, raised his eyebrows apologetically, unpeeled the tight black glove, and offered it again. She took it instinctively. At Whitethorn good manners became instinctive in order that snubs should be purposeful.

'Where is Leo?' She looked round absurdly, as though expecting him to rise from the trench. Not that that was impossible. In the right mood he was capable of anything.

'There's a fishing party organized up the water a ways. Satisfaction guaranteed, I believe. Trout leaping into your bucket.'

'Leo *fishing*?' said Zeugma. 'What about his work?'

It came out rather more bitterly than she intended.

'He's been feeling guilty about you,' Upas assured her. 'We all have. I was sorry I missed you at the pub yesterday so I thought I'd ride over here today and see if I could spot you. I do a bit of scrambling and trials riding too when I get the chance and this bit of countryside's the perfect practice course.'

It was not a way of considering the countryside which Zeugma found much more endearing than Lakenheath's industrial vision. Upas was indicating his bike with some pride, and looking more closely at it even Zeugma's inexpert and uninterested eye spotted one or two modifications to the normal road model. The rear tyre seemed at least twice as wide as the front and looked very flat. The handlebars were high, nothing like so much as 'chopper' bars, but higher than normal. Indeed the whole machine seemed rather higher with several inches more ground clearance than a normal road model, and the wheelbase was noticeably shorter too. The exhaust system was raised. All in all it possessed much of the kind of 'machine-savagery' which sometimes made Zeugma afraid.

'It's basically a Bultaco Sherpa, with a few modifications of my own,' said Upas. 'It's a fine sport. Tests the nerve and keeps you fit. Something like this between your legs over a bit of rough terrain, well, it strains every muscle in your body to keep it under control.'

He glanced at her boldly to make sure she took the innuendo.

'I tend to regard machines as admissions of defeat,' she said. 'Men use them to compensate for their shortcomings.'

'You put it too lightly,' he answered. 'They don't merely compensate. They transcend! Perhaps I'll take you for a ride some time. You'll see! Look, why don't you come up to our little place for dinner? Tomorrow night, say. Better still, bring your kit and stay over. What's sauce for old Leo . . .'

'*Our* place?' enquired Zeugma politely.

Upas frowned at her.

'Well, my brother's really. Malcolm. But it belongs to the family. He just happened to come along thirteen years before me.'

'Malcolm Upas,' said Zeugma, wondering if he were cast in the same mould as his brother. There was something naggingly familiar about Upas. Omar Shariff, perhaps. Or Sheikh Yamani. She hoped that perhaps first impressions could sometimes be trusted after all.

'Yes. What time shall I call on you?'

Their discussion was interrupted by another arrival.

The wolf-dog bounded into the dip, ignored the human beings entirely, but paused to cock its leg against the motor-bike.

'Sod off!' said Upas amiably, swinging his boot at it. The dog evaded the blow easily and its red-tinged eyes flickered momentarily over Upas's frame as though, it seemed to Zeugma, deciding which jawful of flesh to tear out first.

'Twinkle!' rapped a stern voice, and the dog backed slowly away, growling softly in its throat as the strangely clad runner appeared over the ridge.

'My God!' said Upas, staring in amazement at this apparition.

'I'd prefer you didn't kick my dog,' said the man. His voice was harsh and guttural, as though speech did not come easy.

'I'd prefer your dog did not pee on my property,' rejoined Upas. 'And though you may know no better than to appear before a lady in your underwear, at least you ought to know how to control a mangy, flea-bitten, sheep-worrying cur.'

The dog's unceasing growl rose a semi-tone.

'Twinkle's no sheep-worrier,' denied the man.

'No? Well, I can believe that. I can't see a dog called Twinkle worrying anything, not even sheep,' mocked Upas. 'Look at him! What's he good for?'

'I race him,' said the man.

'Race him?' Upas was genuinely amazed. 'What in? He's not a hound; they don't let you enter him for trials, do they?'

'I mean, I race against him. Over the moors.'

Now Upas was really interested. He scents a bit of sport, thought Zeugma.

'To what end?' enquired Upas. 'And who wins? How can the beast know it's a race?'

'He knows,' said the man grimly. 'And he makes sure he always wins. There's nought to beat him on these moors. Man, beast. Or machine.'

He looked scornfully at the motor-bike. And Zeugma suddenly had a sense that he was dangling a bait.

'You're joking,' said Upas, following his gaze. 'Will it race me? On this?'

He pulled the bike upright.

'Ay. If I tell him to.'

'And what would be the wager? I only race for money. Can you manage a tenner?'

It was a lie. Zeugma could see that Upas was determined to race whatever happened. The introduction of the money factor was merely an attempt to make the man back down from his certainties.

Quickly she spoke.

'I'll put up Twinkle's tenner.'

Upas grinned at her. He was really very attractive despite everything.

'A sportswoman too. Fine. Now what's the mark? It must be mutually agreed. I want no fifty-yard sprint!'

The man cast an assessing eye round the countryside and pointed north.

'Yon grove of elders.'

The trees he was pointing at were a quarter of a mile away, too far for Zeugma to essay on identification but the only ones in sight in that direction.

Upas examined the terrain between carefully. He was no longer smiling and he no longer looked like the young city gent, patronizing the peasantry. He looked like a professional, weighing all things carefully in the probability scales. It was not a change that was altogether for the better.

To Zeugma's eye, which under Leo's tutelage had developed a certain skill in assessing the characteristics of landscape, the odds seemed very much in Upas's favour. Twinkle would be able to take the more direct route but nothing in the gently undulating moorland seemed to demand an excess of circumnavigation from a skilled motor-cyclist. Upas clearly arrived at the same conclusion.

'There and back?' he said. 'You're on.'

He climbed on the motor-bike, started the engine first time and drew the goggles down over his eyes.

'You say the word,' he said to the man. 'So the hound understands.'

The man snapped his fingers and when Twinkle came to him he stooped and spoke softly in the dog's ear.

Upas grinned confidently at Zeugma, the man stood up and said, 'You ready?'

Upas nodded, the man said quietly, 'Right, Twinkle,' and the dog was away. Upas who had been expecting something rather more dramatic was left standing at the post, but he quickly recovered, resisted the temptation to over-throttle and smartly pulled away. In twenty seconds he was up with the dog and in another twenty he was leaving it well behind.

'He's a fair rider,' said the man unworried.

'Yes, he is. I'm a bit worried about my tenner,' said Zeugma.

'No need. I'll stand the gain or the loss myself,' he replied brusquely, adding, as if to soften the harshness, 'Not that he'll lose.'

'You seem very confident, Mr . . . ?'

'Crow.'

'Mr. Crow. Tell me, how on earth does Twinkle know where to go?'

'He's a bright dog,' Crow answered. 'Even with a name like Twinkle.'

Zeugma, whose own strange name had once caused her many embarrassments, asked with interest, 'Why did you call him that?'

'Who'd think he could be beat by a dog called Twinkle?' answered Crow.

Musing on this, Zeugma returned her attention to the race. Upas was still ahead, but the dog was now holding its own. The bike had been slowed down by a patch of close-growing grassy tummocks and was now pursuing a course at right angles to the flying crow line.

Perhaps, thought Zeugma hopefully, perhaps the terrain will force a very long detour, but the thought was hardly formulated before Upas wrestled the front wheel round and began heading straight for the trees once more. For about thirty yards he accelerated, then with dramatic suddenness he slowed and the wheels span, sending great gobbets of sludge into the air.

'Is there a bog there?' asked Zeugma.

'Looks like it,' said Crow phlegmatically.

Upas had to dismount and drag his deeply buried

wheels out by main force. He had kept the engine going, however, and he quickly remounted and began to move slowly to the right athwart an uphill slope, scanning the ground carefully in search of a safe route.

Twinkle was now in the lead, loping steadily forward with an ugly but ground-consuming gait. Upas suddenly turned the bike round and began running back down the slope. He had realized, Zeugma guessed, that there was no relationship between height and bogginess on these moors. You could scale the highest point and still sink up to your calves.

Twinkle reached the trees at the same time that Upas at last found a route which circumvented the bog. Crow pursed his lips in what might have been a soundless whistle and the dog began the return journey passing within a yard of the man as he sent the bike bucking and bouncing up the slope to the grove. By the time he reached the first tree, conscientiously reached out and touched it, then wrenching the heavy machine round for the return journey, Twinkle had a lead of nearly two hundred yards. It seemed a winning margin.

But Upas was no easy loser, Zeugma realized. He knew the route now, and he had the kind of mind which kept hold of things. And above all he was not afraid of risks.

The note of the motor-bike engine changed, ran up half an octave, broadened into a chord and the sleek machine began to accelerate down from the trees at a breakneck speed.

Zeugma glanced at Crow who seemed to be talking to himself or perhaps he was murmuring some sub-aural encouragements to his beast. The machine was closing fast on the animal. Upas's handling was masterly and despite her economic support for the dog, Zeugma had to respond to the supple strength and grace of the man's control. It was like watching a fine jockey at work, but more than that, for a horse has a rhythm in its running that a rider can learn and respond to, while this assemblage of metal and rubber reacted violently to every dip and knoll.

He caught the dog with fifty yards to go. Crow had stopped muttering. Zeugma felt almost ready to cheer. The bike drew ahead. Out of the grass directly in front of it started a hare.

Upas leaned the bike on its side in a manoeuvre which on a track and at twice the speed might have slid him safely round the obstacle in a flurry of cinder. Here on the tussocky grass there was no chance. He almost got away with it for all that, but at the last minute had to thrust the bike away from under him to avoid getting his leg trapped as its forward momentum failed and it subsided like a shot stag to the ground.

The hare hopped unhurriedly away, passing close to Twinkle who gave it what might have been a promissory glance but came straight on.

Crow nodded approvingly at it but said nothing and the dog lay at his feet, baring its yellowed teeth as it panted slightly from its exertions.

'Are you all right?' called Zeugma as Upas approached, pushing the bike. He nodded, smiling. Whitethorn approved a good loser and Zeugma smiled back sympathetically.

'Hard luck,' she said. 'What a pity about that hare.'

'Yes indeed,' he said. 'I thought I was only racing the dog, Mr Crow.'

'We've all to thole our weird, Mr Upas,' said Crow harshly. 'Twinkle!'

He turned away.

'Wait,' said Upas. 'I owe you money.'

'The lass put up the stake. You pay it to the lass.'

'That sounds fair,' said Upas. 'But the dog deserves something surely.'

From his belt he pulled a short slender branch still freshly green where it had been torn from the tree.

'Proof that I reached the grove,' he said. 'Perhaps your

dog would like it to play with.'

Crow looked at the branch for a long half-minute. So, thought Zeugma with a Pasquino-like flash of vision, must the priest of the sacred grove have regarded the latest pretender to his post, knowing that death alone could settle the claim.

'You keep it till I need it,' Crow said finally. 'Twinkle doesn't fetch sticks.'

Then he broke into the low loping stride so reminiscent of the dog's and the two of them ran off to the north.

Zeugma watched them go, till the noise of the motor-bike engine startled her. Upas too was ready to make an abrupt departure.

'Eight o'clock tomorrow evening,' he said to her. 'Be ready.'

'Wait. I haven't said . . .'

'Debts must be paid,' he interrupted. 'Till eight!'

It was no use shouting into the roar of his exhaust and he didn't have a rear-view mirror so even the abusive sign Zeugma sent after him was wasted.

Soon the engine sound had died away. Crow and Twinkle were now out of sight. Her only company lay beneath her. The dead. And even the dead were no longer totally reliable these days.

With a sigh whose source she did not altogether understand, she bent down and began unfastening the tarpaulin which she had drawn protectively over her excavations. She drew it back with her usual care till half the trench was revealed. Then with growing excitement and incredulity she hastily dragged it completely clear and stared down into the hole, unable to comprehend what she saw.

The bones had returned.

6

*How the bulk of a man should sink into
so few pounds of bones and ashes may
seem strange unto any who considers not
its constitution . . .*

The wind grew stronger and colder. It was a wind to send most generously furred and blubbered animals to their folds, earths, warrens and caves. Lakenheath was discovering that even the long-practised Scots had not really learned how to fight the weather. A tartan rug over a Harris tweed jacket over a Fair Isle sweater was proving to be much less efficacious than a rabbit's fur.

Below, nothing had stirred since Zeugma had left him here over an hour earlier. This did not surprise him. A series of covered ways connected all the buildings and from Lakenheath's position only movement in the open or at the windows nearest to him would be visible.

His back was aching, he felt stiff and cold all over. He pulled the rug closer about him and shivered violently. Why, he asked himself, why am I sitting up here freezing when I could be in my hotel room, supping whisky and waiting for that insolent little chambermaid to come and make the bed? Scottish cloth may have failed me, but the nation has other sources of warmth.

He glanced at his watch. He had not made any firm agreement about the time of Zeugma's return and he suspected she was capable of leaving him up here till nightfall. Or later.

Movement was necessary, he decided, if he were to deny her the pleasure of finding him petrified between earth and sky.

He rose, leaning heavily on his shooting stick till he was able to balance on his good foot, and began hopping around, arms waving, with what vigour he could muster.

At that moment two figures appeared at the gate of the centre and raised their faces towards him.

Without his binoculars it was not possible to work out if he had been spotted. They might be just casting pseudo-rustic glances at the sky. Or if they had seen him, they might take him for some local village idiot performing a fertility dance.

He sat down so that the crest of the ridge concealed him from view. This had been a stupid idea, he thought. It could produce nothing except perhaps pneumonia. There was rain in the wind now and with no guarantee of how long it would be before Zeugma returned, he would do well to start seeking his own salvation.

Carefully he rose to his feet and began to move down-hill, making for the road. If the visitors had gone, he would seek shelter in the centre; if they hadn't, then he would forget embarrassment, concoct some story to explain his presence and beg a lift back to Brampton. This was his intention but when, as he hopped down the last stretch of grass alongside the gatehouse, he heard a car engine cough into life like a septuagenarian smoker on a cold morning, some irresistible instinct made him fall to the ground and press himself into the damp earth for concealment.

When he looked up, the Morris Oxford was disappearing down the road.

'Damn!' he said. 'Damn!'

On the other side of the road something moved, just enough to catch his eye. It was a rabbit and after this one little hop, it sat quite still, only an intermittent twitch of the ears showing it was a living creature. Such intrepitude in so timid a creature interested him and he slowly rose and started to hobble across the road. The rabbit still did not move. 'Perhaps,' mused Lakenheath aloud, 'perhaps you are someone's pet. What's your name then? Hey, hey – Fluffy.'

There was a loud explosion and now Fluffy moved. Its belly was ripped open in a tatter of blood and flesh and the small creature was hurled backwards two or three feet before coming to rest with a stillness that made its previous quietude seem turbulent.

'Jesus wept!' exclaimed Lakenheath, spinning round on his good foot.

In the gateway of the centre, with a smoking shotgun in his hand, stood Diss. Behind him, invisible from the ridge, was the Buick.

'What the hell are you playing at?' demanded Lakenheath, furious to find he was shaking.

Diss stared silently at him, if it could be called a stare that showed so little interest.

Finally he spoke very softly in what sounded like a foreign language. Lakenheath could not catch what he said.

'What?' he asked.

'Myxomatosis.'

Lakenheath turned and peered down at the remains of the rabbit. Its head which had survived untouched, was swollen and covered with sores. No wonder it had been sitting so still.

Diss had come to stand beside him and the shotgun barrel ran between them like a hand rail.

'Fortunate you carry a gun in your car,' said Lakenheath.

Diss inserted another cartridge and snapped the barrel back into place.

'You never know when it might come in handy,' he

64

said. 'Now let's talk. You look weary. I'll fetch the car.'

He walked into the centre and left Lakenheath to contemplate the remains of the rabbit. He had seen plenty of dead animals, even shot a few in his time though as a sport he felt it fell a long way short of table tennis. But he had never been so close to a creature at the moment of impact. His memory kept on re-running the incident in slow motion so that he saw the smoking swarm of pellets burrow and burn their way through the rabbit's fur, saw the small body expand like an inflatable toy till finally it burst and the spheres of lead re-emerged in a nebula of blood and flesh.

It was a comfort when the Buick ran silently alongside him and Diss motioned him to climb in. No man would want a mess like that in his own car.

Diss himself climbed out, pulled the centre gates to and locked them.

'I promised Mr Sayer I'd see everything was safely locked,' he said on his return. 'He seemed most concerned that the place shouldn't be overrun with intruders. No hippy communes, that kind of thing.'

'He told you about that!' exclaimed Lakenheath indignantly.

'I'm afraid so. Not to suggest inefficiency on your part, I may add, just as general information. Indeed, if he knew you were here now, he would be impressed as I am by your devotion to duty. Injured though you are, you still come out here in the wilds to assist your colleague. On foot too.'

There was no hint of irony in his tone, but there didn't need to be.

'I got a lift,' said Lakenheath. 'And it wasn't to help Sayer I came. Bird-watching.'

He tapped his binoculars. Diss nodded approvingly.

'I like a man with a feel for nature. This is fine country.'

As he spoke his gaze passed slowly over the rolling moorland, empty except for the dark geometric shapes of conifer plantations, scattered like pieces of a child's jigsaw on a grey-green counterpane. The sky was indeed huge but very dark now. The clouds must still have been ripping along at a smart pace before the unremitting wind, but the cover was almost too solid for the movement to be remarked.

'What brought you here in the first place, Mr Lakenheath?' enquired Diss. 'The scenery?'

'The job, Mr Diss,' replied Lakenheath calmly. 'What about you? What are you doing here?'

'Me? I'm just a businessman looking for *lebensraum*,' said Diss.

Lakenheath gave a disbelieving snort which self-interest then tried to turn into a cough. It sounded unconvincing, but then another sound reached them, very distant and almost drowned by the wind which bore it.

'Is there a quarry close by?' enquired Diss.

Lakenheath did not reply but pointed straight ahead. Momentarily the wind had torn a rift in the clouds through which the sun now trailed a sheet of light, its edges grey and tattered and even its central radiance stained by an oblique column of smoke.

Diss switched on the engine and the Buick accelerated away in one powerful smooth movement. Lakenheath felt himself infected by an illogical urgency as the big car ate up the long straight stretch of road which ran away from the centre. It wasn't till they rounded the first bend required by the contours of the land that they saw anything.

A few hundred yards ahead a burning car lay on its side by the road. A black-clad figure shielding his face with one hand was trying to drag the car door open with the other, but the fury of the flames was driving him back. Even though the flames were running the whole length of the car, Lakenheath recognized it.

'Oh Christ!' he said. 'Sayer!'

The man in black made another approach as they pulled to a halt and Diss leapt out and dragged him back. He was wearing gauntlets and a motor-cyclist's helmet which had afforded him some protection from the fire, but clearly the heat was impenetrable.

Another vehicle came tearing cross country from the left. It was a jeep and a tall bearded man whom Lakenheath recognized as Jenkins, a local Forestry Commission worker, jumped out with a fire extinguisher which he began to play on the burning car. The jeep driver meanwhile could be heard on his radio giving details of the accident to his control.

Diss now produced a small extinguisher from the Buick and added his efforts to Jenkins' while Lakenheath helped the motor-cyclist to the side of the road where his bike lay.

'Are you okay?' he asked.

'A bit charred, I think,' said the man. 'But nothing much. It was terrible, I couldn't get him out.'

'What happened?' asked Lakenheath.

'I don't know. I wasn't on the road myself. I was doing some scrambling practice up there when I heard the bang. He must have blown a tyre, gone off the road and turned over. The car was blazing by the time I got to it.'

He sat with his head bent down between his knees and took several deep breaths. He was only a youngster, Lakenheath saw, and the shock must have been great.

The extinguishers had done their jobs, he observed, and the flames were now out, but the car still glowed and smoked making anything but a visual examination impossible. That this was enough was apparent from Jenkins' face as he peered in through the heat-shattered windscreen. He came across to Lakenheath shaking his head.

'It's no good,' he said. 'My God, Mr Lakenheath, I thought it must be you when I saw what car it was.'

Beside him the young man stirred and Jenkins bent to examine him.

'Hang on,' he said and went to the jeep where Diss and the driver were in conversation. He returned with a first-aid box and after carefully easing the scorched gauntlets off began to anoint the boy's hands and face.

'That was a brave thing you did,' he said. 'You nearly got him out. We saw from the edge of the plantation up there. If we could have come straight down with the extinguishers we might have saved him, but there's a bloody stream in the way.'

'He's dead then?' asked the youth.

'I'm afraid so. Never mind. You did your best. What's your name? I've seen you riding around before on that bike, haven't I?'

'Possibly. I'm Jonathan Upas. I live up in Liddesdale.'

Lakenheath looked up with interest at this information. So this was one of the fat girl's Upases. But it wasn't the time for an exchange of small talk.

'You did well,' he said, rising, and limped to the jeep.

'They've raised the police and the ambulance men,' said the driver whom Lakenheath also knew slightly.

'You know,' he went on, unconsciously echoing Jenkins, 'for a moment when I saw the car, I thought it must be you in it, Mr Lakenheath.'

'No,' said Lakenheath unnecessarily. 'No. Not me?'

He felt Diss's gaze on him and met it unwaveringly.

'It was lucky you took your own car, Mr Diss,' he said. 'Or you might have been in the Morris too. By the way, you never did say why Sayer left the centre before you did.'

'I believe he had an urgent appointment,' replied Diss.

'An appointment,' echoed Lakenheath.

He sat down by the roadside again despite the fact that it was beginning to rain in earnest. The fat drops sizzled against the hot metal of the burnt-out car and no one spoke until they heard distantly the oncoming sirens of the ambulance and police car.

7

Bones, hairs, nails, and teeth of the dead,
were the treasures of old Sorcerers.

Zeugma after sitting on the edge of her trench for half
an hour musing on the returned bones and tangential
mysteries of Crow and Twinkle, Pasquino and Upas,
Lakenheath and Diss, decided finally that this was no
way for a Whitethorn product to behave. Looking into
yourself was one thing; irritably reaching after fact and
reason in the midst of uncertainties and mysteries was
something quite different. Experience had taught her that
whenever she felt bewildered (occasionally), outraged
(frequently), or menaced (nearly all the time), the best
anodyne was hard work.

The home-coming skeleton was complete save for the
left hand. Interesting also was the manner of death, which
seemed to have been violent, the rib-case and the skull
showing signs of having been pierced by thrusts from a
sword or spear. A theory began to form in her mind and
she began to work with a will. And so successful was this
as an antidote to the problems and cares of the world at
large that when she at last rose to the surface of conscious life, flushed with exertion and with triumph in
having conclusively proved (to herself at any rate) that
this was a disposal pit for the carcases of executed soldiers,
she was amazed to find how much time had gone by. It
was late afternoon, the sky had succumbed wholly to the

cohorts of cloud being spurred in from the west and the wind which had been piously tiptoeing round the exhumation hollow jumped out and grabbed her with unsuspected violence when she abandoned the shelter of the grave. There was rain in the gusts now, thin strands so icily cold that they fell across the skin like white-hot filaments.

Lakenheath! she thought. A severe cold was no more than he deserved, but death from exposure was too high a price even for deliberate ill-manners.

Pausing only to ensure that her excavations were firmly topped with the sheet of canvas, she set out through the untimely gloom at a speed a little beyond that of safety. When she reached the knoll on which she had left Lakenheath, a glance was enough to tell her he was no longer there, but she still got out of the Range Rover and climbed up to the spot.

Below her Thirlsike Research Centre lay. Deserted buildings have an unmistakable look, she thought. Like a lost child on a beach. Or the pale face of a condemned man being led to the place of execution.

She started, surprised to find such an uncharacteristically grisly thought coming into her mind. It must be the dig. Could it possibly be a burial place for executed criminals? She no longer felt certain and wished she could talk to Pasquino about it.

She shook him out of her mind. Tomorrow night she would be seeing him once more. Lakenheath was her present concern. Could he have clambered down the slope and sought shelter in the centre? Quickly she returned to the Range Rover and sent it bucketing over the rough terrain towards the road.

The huge metal gate suspended between smooth concrete posts was locked. Nevertheless she peered between the bars and called out.

'Hello! Mr Lakenheath! Are you there?'

There was no reply, but she thought she sensed a movement somewhere in the complex of buildings. It would be surprising of course if there weren't living things inside. Birds, rats, foxes even. She squinted through the bars once more.

She had never been inside, but knew something of the history of the place from listening to Charley in the Old Kith. The grey stone building she could see almost straight ahead must be the old fever hospital. What a place to be brought to! And not in an ambulance over a metalled road, but on a farm-cart, drawn by plodding horses over a rutted and broken track. What hope could anyone have had of return? It was a relief to get back into the Range Rover and back away from the gates.

What now? she wondered. Coming out with me on the moors is clearly the kiss of death.

The thought was grimly humorous but also extremely disturbing. Suppose the half-wit had set off to follow her and got lost? At least he wouldn't have been able to get very far with his sprained ankle.

For the second time in three days she found herself driving across the bare and treacherous waste in search of a lost companion. This time she was more systematic, describing as far as the land contours would permit her a zigzag search pattern and stopping at each turning point to shout and listen.

Her search was taking her west and north, which seemed the most likely directions he would have strayed in. Worry and anger warred in her mind.

When I find the idiot, she thought furiously, I'll kill him!

And then the answer would come that perhaps there would be no need.

The rain was now coming down in real earnest, no longer in fine filaments but with the brutal and unavoidable lash of a cat-o'-nine-tails. It was getting very dark also and the cloud cover was growing thicker and lower all the time. Even if she headed straight to the nearest telephone now, it was going to be difficult to get any properly organized search going in time. On the other hand, she thought with grim humour, she might find a message waiting for her saying that Lakenheath too had gone to stay with the Upases in Liddesdale.

One more sweep. She halted, sounded a couple of blasts on the horn, reversed, flicking the headlights on and off as she did so, then climbed out and shouted.

Once again as at the centre she sensed a movement She shouted again and this time got a fix on it; to her right and down a steep declivity out of which grew some close-set and incredibly hardy whins. It was probably just a rabbit, but the chance that Lakenheath might be lying there, injured and half-conscious, sent her scrambling down the slope to investigate.

Halfway down she clung tightly to a fistful of the thin branches and leaned out to peer into the shadows below. The rain ran down her neck, her slacks clung damply to her legs, and even her anorak was rapidly surrendering to the ferocious onslaught.

'Anyone there?' she called.

The answer came from behind. A heavy weight crashed on to her back, she felt a length of flesh and muscle grapple her close to itself, hot breath burnt on her neck as she tried to twist round. She shrieked and released her grip and she and her assailant rolled down the slope in a furious tangle of limbs and sodden whins. Her head struck something solid and the strength ebbed from her body. There was no way she could resist.

Then a stern voice spoke, like God from a cloud.

'Twinkle!' it said. 'Heel!'

Crow hardly fell over himself to be apologetic. Indeed the only words of explanation he offered were, 'He keeps a good watch.' But some actions speak louder than some words and when the man led her unresisting to the dwelling place so ferociously guarded by Twinkle and gave her an earthenware drinking bowl filled with a thick, sweet, powerful liquid, Zeugma felt herself adequately compensated.

Even though she had come close enough to Crow's house to merit Twinkle's attentions, she doubted if she would have noticed it without his guidance. It was a single-storey dry-stone structure, its interstices plugged with turf and moss and the whole set into a hillside so that it was hard to tell where the natural ended and the man-made began. It was built in the style of a medieval long-house. There was a central living chamber with a corner hearth well placed so that little of the peat smoke drifted into the room. Off this were two other rooms separated from the main chamber only by a kind of arch or buttress in the walls. It was too dark to see what they contained. The one to the right in the traditional medieval set-up ought to have been a byre. She would have been surprised to find cattle on this part of the waste, but certainly a distinctly animal odour pervaded the place. Crow's sleeping berth she surmised was the broad slab of stone jutting out of the wall by the hearth like a crusader's niche in a church. The chair she sat on was stone too, but covered with a comfortable rug of soft pelts.

Zeugma took another long pull at her bowl and screwed up her eyes and opened her mouth in exquisite pain as the golden mixture trickled like sweet lava down her throat.

'What is this?' she asked when the anaesthetic effect had worn off her vocal cords.

'Whisky and honey mainly,' Crow said. 'Athole Brose, the North British call it.'

If he had said 'ambrosia' she would not have been surprised.

'It's jolly good,' she said inadequately. 'You must give me the recipe.'

'You're soaked through,' he said abruptly. 'Better get out of those clothes.'

73

'No, no, I'm fine,' she said uneasily. 'I'll just steam dry here.'

He laughed, a noise like a magpie's call.

'Do as you will,' he said. 'Or as you must.'

Something almost scornful in this last remark got to Zeugma. She took another draught from the bowl.

'All right,' she said, rising. 'Where?'

He jerked his head towards the shadowy right-hand chamber.

'There are some blankets there,' he said.

There was no door to close behind her, but the rough buttresses provided some protection and after checking that Crow remained sitting on his bed-slab peering into the fire, she quickly removed her clothes. Her eyes were becoming used to the light and she had no difficulty in finding the blankets which were stored in a kind of open stone dresser built on the Stonehenge principle of pillars supporting cross pieces. The blankets were rough-woven with an intricate patern of red foliage curving through the light grey background. The harsh wool made her skin glow as she towelled herself down with a vigour that Miss Akenside would have approved of.

It seemed silly to exchange wet clothes for a damp blanket, so she draped the makeshift towel over a stone projection and helped herself to another blanket.

Something fell to the ground as she pulled it off the shelf. She stooped and picked it up.

It was a shoe. Left foot. Tan suède. In need of some repair at the heel. Caked with dry mud. Size four. A woman's shoe. She smiled. So Crow was human, after all.

Tucked inside the shoe was a nylon stocking and a piece of newspaper; to hold the shape while drying, Zeugma thought at first. But it was not bundled up, just folded and laid inside the shoe. Curiously, she unfolded it.

It was a cutting from an eighteen-month-old copy of the *Cumberland News*. It contained an account of an inquest into the death of a Brampton girl, Sharon Anderson, whose naked body had been discovered a few days earlier near Bewcastle.

Discovered by a man called Crow. The account of the inquest was thorough, almost verbatim. Clearly such a treat came but rarely to the good people of Cumberland.

The cause of death had been asphyxiation. Bruising round the face and traces of woollen fibres in the nose, mouth and lungs led the pathologist to suggest person or persons unknown had held the girl's head beneath a woollen article, possibly a blanket, till she had died.

She had also been beaten across the shoulders and buttocks with a solid but supple weapon, possibly a thin branch of willow or similar wood, hard enough to raise weals but not draw blood.

She was not a virgin, but there were no signs that she had had sexual intercourse, either willingly or forcibly, in the hours prior to her death.

But, the pathologist had added with justifiable pride in his craft, she _had_ eaten a substantial meal of wild duck and drunk a great deal of alcohol, probably whisky, within two or three hours or being smothered.

Zeugma burped gently, an uncontrollable reaction of hers when frightened, and tasted the Athole Brose in her mouth. The shoe weighed heavily in her hand. Angrily she thrust it back to the rear of the shelf. It was only a shoe, after all. A common man-made thing.

But her hand now touched something that felt less familiar, less everyday. Carefully she pulled the new find to the front of the shelf and peered at it in the dim light filtering from the main chamber. And immediately wished she hadn't.

Before her lay a hank of blonde hair and a little pile of small bones.

'Come back to the fire,' commanded Crow suddenly, and she started, almost displacing the bones from the shelf. Hastily she thrust them back and, with trembling heart, she drew the blanket so tightly around her that the rough fibres scratched her skin, then returned to the fire and sat down.

Instantly Crow rose and towered over her, one half of his long, lean face lit up by the fire's glow, the other half in shadow. She felt her body tense itself for struggle, but he merely turned, went to the end of the building and after a moment came back with her wet clothes which he draped over a length of rope which stretched across the fireplace.

After that he sat down once more and looked at her in silence for some minutes, a silence Zeugma felt herself unable to break.

'What brought you to my dwelling?' he asked abruptly. 'Something to be dug up for the old bones it contains?'

'No!' she protested. 'It was an accident. I had no idea. Really? Anyway, what I'm doing is preserving things in a way, giving new life to the past.'

The banality made her squirm, but she felt a desperate need to keep the conversation at the level of a discussion of her work. What else there might be to dig up in this house she did not know. Nor did she wish to find out just now.

The drinking bowl had been replenished and she poured a quarter pint down her throat before she realized what she was doing.

'New life?' he said harshly. 'Those poor criminals have found their peace. Eighteen hundred years is not long to forget such suffering. Not long. Though for others the suffering was greater and the waiting is just beginning.'

His eyes were almost closed as he spoke these enigmas and even the heat generated in her belly by the honeyed brose could not prevent Zeugma from shivering as she gazed at the ageless face, drawn and still like a death-mask, which the light of the flickering fire scarcely seemed to touch.

How long they sat like this was hard to say. Ten minutes, twenty, half an hour. The drinking bowl lay invitingly beside her, but she did not care to taste any more. Outside the wind raged and screamed still, rising to a pitch of agonized sound which it seemed must be produced from a human throat.

Suddenly she recalled her actual purpose in wandering round the moors in this foul weather and overcome by guilt and dismay she exclaimed, 'Lakenheath!'

'What?' The exclamation seemed to bring him out of his coma.

'That's why I came,' she gabbled. 'I was with someone, not the man you saw me with, Upas, not him, but somebody else before I saw you, if you understand. Lakenheath. Oh, he's an awful man and he wants to build factories all over the waste, but he's got a sprained ankle and I'm worried in case he's got lost somehow and is in trouble somewhere.'

She rose suddenly, angry with herself for losing precious minutes of light. A sound like a distant saw-mill made her freeze. Twinkle in his corner was growling gently as he watched her with much suspicion. His sagacious eye was a long way from owning an inmate.

Crow leaned forward and poked the fire with an ash stick. A peat turf fell apart, revealing its glowing heart like the flesh of a pomegranate. He peered into it as though into a book.

'No,' he said finally. 'Be easy. There's none that suffers on the waste this moment. Though suffering there has been this day. Great suffering.'

Zeugma eyed him dubiously.

'Yes. Well,' she said. 'I still think I'd better be going, if you don't mind.'

If Twinkle doesn't mind, she really meant.

Crow glanced at the dog and smiled a positive identifiable smile this time. 'Twinkle,' he admonished. 'Miss Gray is a friend. Friend.'

The dog went to sleep. It looked as if it was smiling too.

Zeugma grabbed her almost dry clothes, retired to the shadows once more and dressed with an anti-productive haste. Crow still did not move from the fire, merely glancing up at her as she returned fully clothed.

'Thank you for the drink,' she said formally. 'Goodbye.'

He did not answer but nodded once and returned his gaze to the fire.

Turn you blind and give you potted-meat legs, thought Zeugma, remembering a favourite warning of her Whitethorn housemistress.

She did not utter it aloud, but left. The blast which hit her as she stepped out of the house felt like the welcoming caress of a friend. It wasn't until ten minutes later as she directed the Range Rover carefully through the sodden gloom that she paused to wonder among all the other mysteries how Crow had also come to the conclusion that the bodies in her trench had been cast there after a Roman execution in the second century A.D.

8

Oblivion is not to be hired. The greatest part must be content to be as though they had not been . . .

Lakenheath sat on the single hard chair his hotel provided and poured himself a toothglass of Scotch. Next he manoeuvred his injured foot on to the bed and pondered the day's events so deeply that even the appearance of the provocative chambermaid to turn down his coverlet passed unremarked.

He had not been close to Sayer, indeed had never liked the man. One of the complex of reasons for hanging on to this job had been to increase by delay the pleasure of telling Sayer what he could do with it. But the man was dead and the manner of his dying made Lakenheath's reaction more than merely conventional.

In addition he could not put out of his mind the words of Jenkins, the forestry man. *When I saw the car I thought it must be you.* Anyone seeing the car would have thought that. And had it not been for the damage to his ankle, it *would* have been him.

He had Zeugma to thank for that. He stirred guiltily at the thought of her, then dismissed it. She had left him there to freeze. It would serve her right to be a bit worried about his disappearance.

He thought instead of Diss. The man with the gun. The last man to talk to Sayer. The last man to be anywhere near the car before the accident.

He shook his head and drank some more whisky. Diss was a bit of a mystery, but shortly he would be someone else's. He was presently at the police station with the Forestry Commission men, giving an account of what they had seen. Jonathan Upas, despite his protests, had been taken to the local hospital to have his burns properly dressed. He had not seemed to like the idea of being a hero and had expressed some concern for his motor-bike which had finally been transported with him in the ambulance. Lakenheath too had been treated gently as an invalid and Sergeant Fell had promised to send someone round to take his statement at the hotel.

There was a knock at the door and Lakenheath thought it must be the police.

'Come in!' he called.

Diss entered, closing the door behind him and taking up a faintly menacing position against the wall.

Lakenheath looked at him with some hostility for a moment, then felt it die. He was in no position either physically or morally to be hostile.

'I've just come from the police station,' said Diss. 'A sad business.'

'Yes,' said Lakenheath. 'Do they know what happened yet?'

Diss shook his head.

'Some mechanical failure perhaps. Or a blow-out. What do you think?'

Lakenheath looked at the other for a long moment.

'Mr Diss,' he said finally, 'there's something I want to say to you.'

It never got said.

The door burst open, pinning Diss behind it and Zeugma made another of her furious entrances. Only this time she was not brightly flushed but very pale.

Her voice had lost none of its soprano indignation, however.

'What the hell's going on?' she demanded.

'I'm sorry. Look, can't it wait?'

'Wait? What for? I want explanations, Mr Lakenheath. I deserve them. It wasn't my idea to take you out on the waste so you could spy on that fellow Diss . . .'

Lakenheath contorted his face warningly, but Zeugma took this merely as a visual threat and continued.

'. . . who by the way is not called Diss, at least not as far as the police are concerned, so he's a fraud to you or them, I don't know which . . .'

Lakenheath's expression now became violent enough to frighten her and she stepped back a pace, permitting Diss to slip from behind the door.

'Miss Gray,' he said with a polite nod. 'Mr Lakenheath. If you'll excuse me.'

He left.

Zeugma for once was speechless.

'You were saying?' prompted Lakenheath.

'I'm sorry,' said Zeugma. 'I didn't know. Look, what's going on? I spent ages looking for you and finally I came back along the centre road and saw a break-down truck with the remains of your Morris hanging from the back of it. Well, I went straight to the police station. They kept me hanging around there for quite a while and I began to get a bit annoyed.'

'No!' interposed Lakenheath. 'Not really?'

'Then Diss came out of a room with Sergeant Fell. Only the sergeant didn't call him Diss but Calgary, something like that. Well, he went off, then I discovered that Mr Sayer had been killed in the accident and I came right round here.'

'Without pause for thought,' said Lakenheath. 'You know as much as me now.'

Briefly he told her of his version of the afternoon's events, skirting round the terrible manner of Sayer's death, and ending with unqualified praise for Jonathan Upas's part in the events on the Thirlsike road.

'Well, well,' she said. 'So he's the hero of the hour. And who's the villain?'

'Sorry?'

'I'm not soft you know, Mr Lakenheath. There *is* something going on, isn't there?'

'I don't know what you mean,' answered Lakenheath, taking another mouthful of Scotch.

'Don't you? You're not going to tell me it's love of your work that sends you crawling across the waste in this weather with a busted ankle! Oh no. I've had some small experience of observing your type, Mr Lakenheath . . .'

'Yes, it would be small,' interposed Lakenheath gently.

'. . . and you feel the world owes you a living and not one that requires any strenuous effort on your part either! So what's going on?'

Why does she get so angry? wondered Lakenheath. Normally she'll just about do; nice and homely, you can imagine her in a farmhouse kitchen with flour on her hands, giggling as some amiable yokel waggles a buttercup under one of her chins. But angry! she's like one of these furious cherubs puffing out the North Wind in some old illuminated map!

'Just what is my type, Miss Gray?' he said aloud, sidestepping her question.

'Type!' she snorted. 'You're an anachronism, a comedian, something out of Wodehouse. Cut you open like a stick of rock and you don't find flesh and blood, you find *public school, Oxbridge, good regiment* printed all the way through!'

Lakenheath was piqued in spite of himself.

'Hold on a sec,' he said. 'You're not quite right in all particulars, you know. In fact, at a glance, I'd say you came a lot closer to that little description than I do. Take school, I went to a South London comprehensive where the going was so rough that even socialist politicians took their children away and sent them to Harrow! I've never been closer to Oxbridge than the M1. And the nearest I ever got to a good regiment was when I stepped out of a taxi into a pile of horseshit in the Mall!'

'Oh,' she said, nonplussed for a moment, then went on: 'If you expect me to retire in confusion, Mr Lakenheath, you'll be disappointed. OK, so you're not the creature I depicted. No, you're worse, because you *pretend* to be him. Still, at least I know I'm dealing with a fraud, which brings me to that other fraud who's just left. Diss alias Calgary. Just which is he? Diss trying to fool the police or Calgary trying to fool you? And why?'

'I'm not really sure, Miss Gray,' he said. 'Couldn't you just have misheard what Fell said?'

'I am not deaf!' she cried with indignation.

'Me neither. But you do get upset, don't you? Why's that? Something to do with your name, perhaps. What possessed your parents to give you such a name. *Zeugma*! But it fits. It means one word incorrectly doing the work of two, and that's you to a T, isn't it?'

'My father wanted me to be distinctive,' said Zeugma coldly.

'God! You must be the apple of his eye now!' laughed Lakenheath.

'My father died when I was fourteen, Mr Lakenheath.'

Lakenheath looked discomfited but Zeugma didn't notice. She was contemplating the justice of his strictures on her. Why she was so agitated by what was patently someone else's problem, she was not sure; something in her make-up needed anger. And she had been given some cause.

'You're evading my question,' she said firmly. 'I've told you that I suspect Diss is a fraud. What are you going to do about it?'

Now he gave a defeated shrug and reached for the bottle again.

'And what would you do?' he asked wearily.

'I don't know. That's up to you,' she said uncertainly.

'Consult Sergeant Fell, I suppose.'

'I see. All right then, I don't suppose it matters much now. Yes, you're quite right about Diss. There's no such firm as Charnell Bearings and whatever slab-face's name is, it's not Mervyn Diss. Satisfied?'

Zeugma's mouth dropped open in a cartoon portrayal of surprise. It was one thing to vehemently propagate a theory, but something else when suddenly without effort it blossomed into a fact.

'Are you sure?' she said. 'I mean, are you sure?'

'I'm sure,' he said, faintly amused at her discomfiture.

'But how, I mean, how did you find out? Did you check with the Directory of Companies or something?'

'No. Nothing so complicated,' he said, getting up from the bed and taking his bottle across to the window. It was still raining heavily.

'Much simpler than that,' he said. 'I knew from the very first moment I saw him that there was no such company as Charnell Bearings and no such person as Mervyn Diss.

'I knew because I invented them in the first place.'

Never sit on a man's bed unless you intend to lie in it, said one of Whitethorn's more memorable dicta, falling (as so many of them did) in a category between etiquette and morality.

A hard chair was just permissible and Lakenheath had vacated his. But Zeugma's podgy knees simply bent like the pink plasticine they resembled and she found herself sitting on the blue-and-yellow counterpane.

'I don't suppose there's any way of getting you out of my room without explaining,' said Lakenheath gloomily.

She shook her head in vigorous confirmation.

'Well, it's simple, really. It's this job, you see. It'll probably please you no end to hear that I haven't done terribly well.'

'If doing it well means bringing in the bulldozers and concrete mixers,' she replied, 'yes, that does please me.'

'Well, it doesn't much please the people who hired me. Sayer in particular.'

The name spread through the room like darkness visible. The rain beat hard against the window-panes and the low-powered bedlight which was the room's only illumination seemed to contract into itself.

'Well, at least he's not worrying any more,' said Lakenheath after a pause. Zeugma felt herself reacting to the apparent callousness of the remark, but held herself in check as she sensed that this was far from the speaker's intentions.

'The thing is, no one seemed much interested in setting up shop here. I don't blame them really. I whipped up a bit of interest when I came here six months ago, but that died down very quickly. Things looked pretty bleak. Poly-fibre, that's Bulstrode's company, the man I was with the first time we met, was the last hope. After that, nothing. Endless days with just me and Miss Peat and nothing to do. Clearly I wouldn't be allowed to continue long on those terms. I needed something in reserve.'

'So you invented Charnell Bearings.'

'Yes.'

'And Diss.'

'Yes.'

'Just so you could keep on getting paid for a job you were not competent to perform.'

'Yes.'

Zeugma got off the bed. She felt quite strong now. In fact she felt her strength was pretty near the strength of six or seven because her reactions were so pure.

'I find that pretty contemptible, Mr Lakenheath,' she said. 'But it doesn't clash with the general picture. You take a contemptible job and in it you behave contemptibly. When this fellow turns up masquerading as Diss, you haven't got the nerve to call him a fraud to his face. You let the game go on, do your pathetic spy act and meanwhile poor Sayer dies.'

'Sayer? That's not my fault,' protested Lakenheath.

'He wouldn't have been on that road if you'd spoken out,' said Zeugma. 'Good-day, Mr Lakenheath.'

'Wait,' he said. 'I haven't finished.'

But she was gone and her gentle closing of the door was somehow more powerfully expressive than the violent exits of the previous day.

Lakenheath stood unmoving for a while, then he knelt, pulled a small suitcase from beneath the bed, unlocked it and gazed down at its contents.

A broken string of beads, a silk stocking, a woman's shoe.

For a moment it seemed the most important thing in the world that Zeugma should return and be made to understand. But the moment passed and she was just a small, plump girl of no consequence again.

In addition there now came another interruption to his attempts to become a solitary drinker. There was a gentle tap at the door.

'Come in!' he yelled, pushing the case back under the bed.

Ten seconds passed and he began to think he had mistaken the noise. Then the door slowly opened.

On the threshold stood Miss Peat.

'I just heard about Mr Sayer,' she said in her slow deliberate manner. 'I thought I should come.'

'Well, that was most kind of you, Miss Peat. Will you step inside?'

Reluctantly she put one foot across the threshold, but the other seemed firmly rooted in the corridor. Slowly her gaze ran round the room, performing a visible ellipsis when it reached the bed.

They all think the worst of me, thought Lakenheath sadly.

'Miss Peat,' he said gently and without hope. 'Do you drink?'

She considered the question.

'Not much,' she said then unexpectedly added, 'except Pernod.'

'Then why don't we go down to the bar and talk about this sad business?' said Lakenheath. Suddenly lonely drinking had lost its attraction. It was that bloody girl's fault. If she would only mind her own business . . . if she *had* minded her own business he might be dead.

'After you, Miss Peat,' he said.

9

While some have studied Monuments,
others have studiously declined them; and
some have been so vainly boisterous, that
they durst not acknowledge their graves.

Zeugma found that a long soak in the Old Kith's even
older bath did a great deal for her physical well-being
and also for her temper. Controlled scorn was even harder
on the nerves than outbursts of fury, and she had felt that
a chat with Charley over a quiet drink in the bar would
nicely round off the repairs. But ten minutes later, she
felt the frayed edges beginning to show once more.

'So you met Crow?' said Charley again.

'Yes,' said Zeugma patiently. She had grown used to
this Cumbrian desire to seek confirmation of every statement made or piece of information given before accepting
or acting upon it, but it wasn't easy.

'On the waste? You met Crow on the waste?'

This was bad, even for Charley, and she thought she
discerned something more here than just the customary
slow and repetitive conversational development. It was
as if before committing himself to any admission of knowledge of Crow, he wanted to make sure she was a fit reci-
pient of such confidences.

'Yes. I met him on the waste. He raced his dog against
a man on a motor-bike and the dog won and I won ten

pounds which I will share with him next time we meet. Then I saw him again in his cottage and we had a long talk and he gave me something to drink, Athole Brose I think he called it.' She repeated the information in a rapid monotone. This seemed to do the trick.

'He's a strange one, Crow,' said Charley knowingly.

'Is he? I've never heard anyone mention him before.'

'No. Well, he's not a man to talk about, not with people he doesn't know or doesn't like.'

So that was it. Charley was afraid of Crow, but at the same time proud of knowing about him. Zeugma settled herself more comfortably on the old well-polished bar-stool.

'How does he live?'

'Oh, he takes care of himself, never fret. Makes a bit of money at the wrestling when he cares to. He's the best round here, which means the best. If he wanted to go off to Grasmere or yon places, he could sweep the board. Wrestling, guide races, anything. And what he didn't win, that dog would!'

'Oh,' said Zeugma, a little disappointed. Crow had struck her as rather more than just a sporting hustler. But Charley was going on.

'He built that house with his own hands, from the bottom up,' averred Charley.

'No,' interrupted Zeugma.

'What?'

'No. There are clear signs of a previous dwelling, I would say. I mean, the very building technique and the interior layout disappeared from vernacular architecture at least three hundred years ago.'

'That's as may be,' said Charley sucking in his beer with some irritation. 'But there was nought there three summers since. No, he moves around, does Crow. Never stays in one spot long. Follows the animals, some say. He'll never starve, that's certain. He can run a rabbit down, or if he can't, Twinkle can. Mark you, if he wanted a chicken or a side of bacon round here, he'd just have to ask. No one would refuse. But he pays his way. Takes nothing locally he doesn't earn.'

'Why would no one refuse?' asked Zeugma. Crow did not strike her as the popular, hail-fellow-well-met type. 'And how does he earn what he earns?'

She could have made a good guess at the answer.

'He's a bad man to be on the wrong side of,' said Charley evasively. 'And he's good with animals, can set bones, lance boils, deliver calves.'

'And?'

'And what?' asked Charley.

'And what else? Can he cast the runes, mix a love-potion, cause a rick-fire or a death? Has he got three nipples and no shadow? Is he the local witch?' She laughed derisively.

Charley downed the best part of a pint without his usual hedonist self-congratulatory closing of the eyes.

'I've work to do,' he said abruptly.

Zeugma was instantly remorseful. It was a mixture of irritation and the three gins she had just consumed which caused her to speak so mockingly.

'I'm sorry, Charley,' she said. 'I didn't mean to offend you.'

'I'm not the one you should worry about offending,' he said grimly.

'You mean, Crow? Well, he won't know I'm chatting about him unless you tell him, will he? Have another pint on me.'

She smiled as she spoke, but when Charley retired to the cool recess in which he kept his cask of best, she found herself glancing uneasily round the shadowy limits of the fire-lit room.

'Wasn't there something about a girl?' she called, to break the silence.

'What?'

'Something about Crow finding a girl's body.'

'Aye, there was,' said Charley returning to the bar. 'But naught was proven.'

'Nothing proven?' she echoed.

'And them as spoke out of turn, they came to no good.' He said it like a warning.

'You mean Crow was under suspicion?'

'He found her and he wouldn't account for his being where she was found.'

'And what do you think, Charley?'

Charley did not answer but, clutching his tankard, retreated into the shadows, so like Marley's ghost that Zeugma would not have been surprised to see the door open of its own accord behind him.

She felt exasperation rising in her again. These men, so naive, so self-obsessed; it was hard to accept them sometimes as part of rational creation.

Crow now – he was something different. But she was far from sure what.

He had done her no harm, in fact shown her nothing but courtesy. Yet the impression that remained was one of strangeness. She was, or imagined she was, quite good at seeing what made people tick (her recent failure with Lakenheath was a misinterpretation of *cause* not of *effect*) but Crow was different. Crow, she had to admit, was frightening. And she could not say why.

It might, she thought as she went through into the kitchen to see what plain delights Charley's taciturn wife had prepared for her, it might be interesting to find out.

Next morning it did not seem in the least interesting. She had a slight headache, having ended the previous night on cherry brandy – possibly, Pasquino used to say, the most revolting drink ever offered to a human being.

She shook him out of her head, winced and set off to the waste to let fresh air and hard work mould her skull back to shape. Once outside however, she did not head straight for her site but on an impulse made a diversion to the nearby village of Bewcastle. Pasquino had escorted her round the ruined castle and the church, both built out of stones remaining from the Roman Fort which had preceded them here. Zeugma recalled Lakenheath's gibe about the locals not being very conservation-conscious either in the past or now.

At least, she told herself, they took what they found and re-used it. It wasn't just a matter of pulverising the past out of existence.

It was to the churchyard that she made her way now, not pausing till she stood before the tall grey column of the famous cross. Pasquino had lectured her on it in his usual informative and idiosyncratic fashion. His interpretation of the runes on the cross's west face, normally taken as a dedication to the memory of King Alcfrith, was radically different from all others, as were his theories on the absence of the actual crosspiece which tradition said had been taken off by a Howard of Naworth and sent to Camden, the historian, in the early seventeenth century. She wished she understood better this need of his to be different. But more important just now was to understand her own needs. Was the feeling of loss she had experienced when he had so unaccountably disappeared merely a gauge of her own uncertainties or was there something more? She had always been aware of the presence in herself of totally irrational fears; her reaction on meeting strangers was usually suspicious, often actively antipathetic, a kind of mild paranoia which was rendered harmless (so she assured herself) by her recognition of it. Upas had been an exception to the rule. Something stirred in her at the memory of the man. Something about him worked a strong charm on her, it was true; but how much was this feeling related to the fact that he had come from Leo?

What I'm really asking myself, she thought firmly is, could Leo and I get married?

There it was and it hadn't been so painful. He was her guardian, but there'd hardly be a law against it. And he was old enough to be her father. Perhaps that's what it had all started from. Her mother she could hardly recall now, even in photographs. But her father was different. Photographs brought him back completely, and also brought back that hideous morning at Whitethorn when, feeling rather pleased that she had been removed from her Latin class before her turn to parse had arrived, she was escorted to Miss Akenside's study and told the news of his death.

No wonder I'm slightly neurotic, she told herself. I'm lucky not to be a raging nut!

She tried to concentrate on the cross. The Old Kith, one theory went, was a corruption of Alcfrith. It could be true. But the hints Charley had dropped about Crow suggested other interpretations!

She walked slowly round the cross, pausing at the south face to peer up at the semi-circular sundial. There was no chance of its working today. The weather was milder and calmer than the day before, but the sky was still overcast. In any case, the gnomon was missing. Doubtless Pasquino would have an original explanation for that too.

He wouldn't leave her thoughts, she realized. So, what were her feelings for him? And what were his feelings for her? She had no points of reference. The only other important emotional relationship in her adult life had been with Hasan in Cairo. When Leo became aware of this, he had definitely disapproved. At the time she had wondered whether a previously concealed racism had come to the surface, but in the end had decided it was merely the age difference between herself and Hasan which bothered him. This wasn't very encouraging now. Hasan had only been ten years older than herself, whereas Leo was twenty. Still, rules were always for other people. She had been very hurt when Hasan had gone away and made

93

no effort to keep in touch. At the time it had seemed like the great love of her life. Looking back at it now, five years later, she wondered how much of it had been this father-thing again. Hasan had known her father during his service in Baghdad and it was this which had first brought them together. Why someone as elegant and worldly wise as he was should have been interested in herself, she couldn't imagine. She had decided then that it was something to do with the special chemistry of love. Now she was able to tell herself dispassionately that Arabs liked their women well fleshed.

Her thoughts refused to concentrate on the main point. Could she, should she, would she marry Leo if he ever asked her? Again she found it impossible to wrestle her mind through to a sensible answer but instead began to do an he-loves-me-he-loves-me-not count of the leaves of the vines with which the east and north faces of the cross were so lavishly decorated. What could Alcfrith and Hwaetred, Wothgar and Olwfwold, have known of vines in this cold northern kingdom?

As much and as little as she knew of herself and her future, came the cold answer from some cavernous depth of her mind.

She turned to go and cried aloud as a figure detached itself from the shelter of a tall weathered headstone and barred her way.

It was Diss. Or Calgary. Lakenheath's absurd invention seemed more apt at the moment. The god of the Underworld.

'Miss Gray,' he said. 'I should like to talk with you.'

She felt as annoyed as if she had discovered a Peeping Tom outside a beach-changing hut.

'I can't see what you can have to say to me,' she said walking past him. He caught her arm.

'You took Mr Lakenheath on to the waste yesterday, Miss Gray. Now why did you do that?'

'It's no damn business of yours,' she said, wrenching

herself free. 'He's a friend of mine. I don't talk about my friends behind their backs.'

She was surprised to find herself claiming friendship with Lakenheath, surprised also to find the comfort it gave to be able to ally herself with alleged hosts of friends. And she needed comfort. Diss no longer held her, but he had moved so that he blocked the path to the church gate.

'You should be careful of your friends, Miss Gray. It's cold standing here. Let's go into the church and have our talk.'

'All right,' said Zeugma, forcing a smile. She turned towards the church, took a couple of steps, felt Diss come alongside, then spun on her heel and dashed down the path, out of the churchyard and into the Range Rover. Only when she was safely inside with the engine started did she look back. Diss, or whatever his name was, had made no attempt to follow her, but stood where she had left him, framed in the arch of the church doorway, his face blank, expressionless, but infinitely menacing.

Suddenly childish again, she thumbed her nose at him, then wrenched the wheel round and drove away. The Buick was parked nearby but she had no fear of pursuit. Where she was going only a fool would attempt to take a long-chassised, oversprung American car.

Five minutes later as she shifted to four-wheel drive and began to make her cautious ascent to the uplands, she started going through that period of self-doubt which seemed to be the inevitable postscript of all her recent actions.

What's wrong with me? she asked herself angrily.

'It's all this looking into myself,' she said aloud. 'Stuff looking into yourself for a lark!'

What she needed was someone else to look into. She was a fool to keep on walking away from people, Lakenheath last night, Diss this morning. She should be nosier; she was naturally nosy, that was what being a historian or an archaeologist was all about; she was happiest when at her nosiest!

She had almost arrived at the excavation sight when a movement on one of the long ridges which ran to the north-west caught her eye. She stopped the Range Rover, took Leo's field glasses out of the glove compartment and brought the moving figures into focus.

It was Crow running alongside Twinkle. They were passing the small clump of trees which had been the mark in yesterday's race. For a moment Zeugma felt a pang of sheer envy at the untroubled joyous ease of motion which the pair so evidently delighted in. Then it died away as it struck her that here indeed was someone who needed looking into.

The discoveries she had made yesterday in Crow's cottage invited investigation. And the more she had thought about it, the more certain she became that the little pile of bones had been the missing hand of her Roman skeleton. So she was personally involved.

With growing excitement she watched the pair out of sight. They must be a good five miles from home and would widen the gap further if they held their present course. She on the other hand could be there in under fifteen minutes.

Today she didn't feel like digging and waiting for things to happen, hourly anticipating the anonymous menace which lay in wait round each corner of her life. Today she was going to sally forth and meet the enemy, whoever he might be, on her own terms. She pressed as hard as she dared on the accelerator. This time there would be no postscript of doubts and regrets. This time . . . !

This time the doubts, regrets and the added bonus of fear came within two minutes of achieving her desired object.

Crow's dwelling seemed to have shifted or her memory of her route the previous day had played her false. And when she finally arrived near the long low building, so easily did it develop and follow the lines and materials of the hillside that she almost didn't see it.

Conscious that she had spent more time getting there than anticipated, she abandoned caution in her approach and marched boldly up to the front door. A hare started from the ground almost beneath the threshold and she stopped in her tracks and a small cry of surprise forced itself through her lips. The animal bounded away for about twenty yards in an easy kangaroo lope, then stopped, sat on its haunches in the classic position with ears pricked, and stared back at her in apparent curiosity. Suddenly she remembered the hare whose unexpected appearance had brought Jonathan Upas off his motorbike.

As if satisfied that he had taken in everything about her, the hare now turned and set off again in a businesslike fashion. He was heading, Zeugma worked out, northwest. To fetch Crow, or so Charley and his superstitious mates would believe, she told herself with a smile she was glad she could not see. It felt a trifle glassy.

The door seemed to have no fastening and when she pushed at the gnarled and weathered wood, it gave way instantly, swinging in as smoothly and silently as the bedroom doors in the Cairo Hilton on the night that Hasan had led her without fuss and without resistance to his room.

Is that ancient history still running through my mind? she asked herself angrily as she stepped inside.

Once over the threshold, she stopped instantly and all memories fled away as she concentrated wholly on the present. It was dark in there, black dark save for what light spilled in through the open door at her back. But it wasn't just the darkness which held her still. Life cannot exist in a confined space without making itself felt, giving itself away. And she sensed a living presence here, something breathing and watching.

She had opened her mouth to speak when there came the beating of what seemed many mighty wings and an angry rasping shriek tore the air. She stepped back, caught her foot on the stone step of the threshold, the polite inanity which had been forming in her mouth came out as a cry of terror, and as she fell backwards some fearful, howling, wing-beating thing brushed past her head and fled into the daylight.

It was just a bird, she told herself as she lay on her back half in, half out of the building and watched the bird rapidly gaining height in the soft grey sky.

No, not *just* a bird, she corrected herself, trying by reasoned observation to still the fearful bells of panic which were still sounding through her mind and down the courses of her blood. A peregrine falcon.

And as if bent on confirming the correctness of her identification, the bird now soared on some column of buoyant air almost directly overhead so that its distinctive anchor shape was clearly apparent. Then it stooped and came hurtling down towards her in a precipitous power-dive; she tried to close her eyes and couldn't, the bird held its dive till it was only ten feet above her head, then it chattered derisively at her from deep in its throat, opened its huge wings and soared away.

She watched it out of sight. It took the same direction as the hare. Suddenly she realized that she probably had very little time. There need be no witchcraft here; if Crow spotted his falcon loose in the sky, he would know instantly that his house had been entered.

Quickly she got to her feet, brushed herself down, took a deep breath, and went back inside.

There was, she rapidly discovered, something very distasteful about poking through other people's belongings. In a paradoxical way, however, it was this distaste which made the business bearable for it occupied her mind to the diminution though not exclusion of her fear, and it was certainly the more resistable of the two evils.

She tried to arrange her thoughts systematically, a task she had found distressingly difficult so far that day.

This man Crow is a mystery. There is something frightening about him. I think he may have stolen my bones. (*My* bones!) I know he was connected with the discovery of a girl's body on the waste and I have seen some articles of female clothing in his house. Therefore ...

... therefore why the hell haven't I come here with a posse of policemen to confront the suspect and have his belongings turned over by professionals?

It was a good clear-cut question. The answer was certainly not quite as clear-cut, and she was not sure just how good it was either. Because, she told herself, because he is, or might be, a free spirit, whatever that is; because he has chosen to separate himself from modern society and all its works; because this separation might be a noble, admirable thing, and because I do not want to be the one who unnecessarily brings the incomprehension of uniforms and the cold heart of officialdom into his life.

Unless I have to.

Her period of thought had given her eyes time to adjust to the dim light and she began her search.

The girl's shoe was on the stone shelf where she had first seen it. She looked at it closely. It was well worn, but still serviceable. Size four, made by a well-known manufacturer. The stocking was still there also, but the hank of hair had been removed.

'Damn!' she said aloud. Shoes and stockings could belong to anybody, but hair was uniquely personal. Well, at least she assumed it was.

She widened the area of her search, though still concentrating on the furthermost section of the building which seemed to be used as a general storehouse. There were rows of earthenware jugs and jars here, most of them filled with liquids and powders. They were unlabelled as

99

far as she could make out in the half-light and thoughts of the ingredients of sorcery began to rise in her mind. Dried blood, powdered toad, essence of hemlock, mandrake root . . . but all a couple of cautious sniffs and even more cautious tastings revealed to her was some coarse flour, some highly spiced vinegar and a large amount of the basic ingredient of the Brose she had drunk the previous day. This was really excellent, pure and resonant in the mouth, clear and glowing in the stomach. She sucked at her finger like a babe at the breast. The taste reminded her of Crow's hospitality and help and she felt a sudden flush of shame at what she was doing.

Carefully she replaced the jug. She wanted to be finished with this business now. There was little else in the storage area; some expertly carved walking sticks, one or two other pieces of wood-carving (but no dolls with nails through their heads, she was glad to note); a pile of rocks and stones, some of the latter semi-precious but unpolished, and several of the rocks bearing small fossils in their surface, leaves, ammonites, that kind of thing.

She returned to the main chamber and cast an unenthusiastic eye round. The steam had gone out of the search; she was no further forward than she had been when she started, all she had got out of the visit were a lot more of those doubts and regrets she had desired to put behind her.

But her trained eye was now focussing more strongly on the actual construction of the building. It was impossible, she told herself, that Crow could have built it from scratch within the last three years as Charley asserted. It must have been a refurbishing job on an extant long-house. But the recessed hearth now . . . that *didn't* fit. It postdated by a couple of centuries the overall style of the place. She might be able to tell something from the markings on the stones where they had been worked.

She approached the hearth and knelt down. The cold

peat ashes stirred gently in the draught from her movement. It was, she thought, a remarkably well insulated house. Many a double-glazed superior modern dwelling let in more cold air than this place. Though it could have done with a bit more light. In fact the light seemed to have perceptibly decreased in the last few seconds. Perhaps it was because the weather had taken a sudden turn for the worse. Or perhaps, she thought as she leaned into the fireplace to get a closer view of the chimney stones, perhaps the main source of light from the door had for some reason become blocked.

And the only reason that suggested itself was that someone was standing there.

She jerked upright at the thought. The back of her head cracked violently against the chimney-lintel and, overcome with giddiness and sickness, she sunk forward till her face rested in the peat ashes and her rasping breath sucked in clouds of choking dust. Through her retching coughs she heard a movement behind her, footsteps approach with slow and deliberate menace. She pushed herself out of the fireplace, turned, through mote-filled eyes mistily saw the tall figure which loomed over her with a club upraised in its right hand, and shrieked.

'You'll need to lose a bit of weight before you can climb up chimneys,' said Lakenheath reprovingly. 'Otherwise you'll just get stuck.'

10

*But many are too early old and before
the date of age.*

Zeugma's tears of pain from the blow on her head,
augmented by tears of relief that it was not Crow who
had discovered her, soon washed most of the ash from her
eyes. She quickly pulled herself together (an activity hopefully consequent on looking into oneself) and essayed a
social smile at Lakenheath who sat on the opposite side
of the fireplace from her, occupying the bed niche Crow
had sat in the previous evening.

'Better?' he said. 'Now, what are you doing here, Miss
Gray?'

There was nothing accusatory in his voice, and though
it might be pleasant to tell him to mind his own business,
it might also be undiplomatic.

'I came to see Mr Crow,' she said. 'I . . . owe him some
money. A bet made on his behalf.'

It wasn't a bad lie, she felt.

'I see. You were putting it up the chimney?' he asked
solemnly.

'Of course not. I was merely examining the construction of the place. I am an archaeologist after all. You
startled me.'

'I'm sorry. You must try not to be so nervous. How's
your head?'

'Bowed but unbloody,' she said. 'And what about you,

Mr Lakenheath? What are you doing here?

'In fact,' she added, looking in surprise at the bandaged foot and the walking stick which rested between his legs, 'how did you get here? Not on foot, surely?'

'No,' he agreed. 'I had a lift. Sergeant Fell brought me as close as he could get, I hopped and slid the rest of the way. The ankle's rather better this morning.'

'I'm pleased to hear it. But why are you here?'

Lakenheath looked at her questioningly for a moment.

'I had a long think after you left yesterday,' he said. 'You know, in a way you were right. If I had challenged that fellow Diss when he first appeared, then poor Sayer wouldn't have been on that road, would he? I'm not going to roll about groaning with guilt and remorse – life's never as simple as that – but I made a mistake and I realize that now.'

'Big of you,' observed Zeugma. 'Well, I'm glad you've got that off your chest and put your conscience at peace.'

'Look,' he said. 'I'm offering an explanation not an apology or a confession. I don't know who may be entitled to those things, but I'm damned certain it's not you.'

This was just, Zeugma had to admit.

'Okay. Carry on. Is there more?'

'Quite a lot. I went to see Fell this morning. He's a sensible enough fellow, though we've had some differences in the past.'

'About parking your car?'

'No,' he said acidly. 'Things more important than that. I accused him and the whole damn police force of being a bunch of shortsighted, inefficient morons a couple of months ago.'

'Oh my! What had they done to deserve such wrath?' she asked.

He was silent for a moment. Suddenly she felt he was wondering whether it was worth continuing talking to her.

'Go on,' she urged.

'Right,' he said. 'You've heard, I think, about the so-called hippy commune which set up in the fever hospital?'

'Oh yes,' she answered. 'Your triumph! Wouldn't the police turn their dogs loose or something as they chivvied them out?'

'They weren't chivvied out,' said Lakenheath. 'Sayer got a bit angry, gave them twenty-four hours to leave. And they left.'

'So it was all Sayer, was it?' she demanded. 'Now he's dead, it can all be Sayer's fault. And while Sayer was out persecuting these people, chucking them out into the cold in the middle of winter, what were you doing, pray? You whose responsibility it all was, you the chief officer of the North East Cumberland Development Council, what did you do for these people?'

'Well,' he said, 'in the first place I gave them the key.'

He was not looking for any point-scoring satisfaction, but he couldn't help but feel a little of it as she sat back in her seat, her eyes rounded with surprise in her smutty face.

'And let's get other things straight,' he continued. 'They weren't a commune. There were only four of them, three women and a man. Travellers they called themselves. They needed somewhere to rest up, get out of the cold.'

'So just out of the kindness of your heart you offered them the research centre?' she said incredulously.

'It wasn't quite just that,' he said quietly. 'No, there were other considerations. Mainly that Julie, one of the girls, is – was – my cousin.'

Oh hell, thought Zeugma lugubriously. Am I going to be proved wrong *again*? But Lakenheath was far from triumph, she realized. He was sitting staring into the cold hearth with eyes that did not see the ashes.

'We were always very close as kids,' he continued. 'We more or less grew up together just a couple of streets apart. Even when she went out of the system and I went into it, we kept in touch. A postcard, a letter, the occasional phone call and sometimes a meeting. She set off drifting early, the usual route I think, London first, then down to St Ives and from there, God knows where. She popped up all over the place. Always looking for the perfect alternative. As I say, I heard from her at fairly regular intervals, occasionally there was even a return address and I could write back. I let her know about my own change of job naturally. Not that she would approve. She's like you in that way. But not in any other. She's tall, very slender, long blonde hair, always looks as if the wind's picked her up and is blowing her along.'

Thanks, thought Zeugma. The unconscious insults are always the worst.

'Last November she turned up here, in Brampton. Just to say hallo, you understand. She never asked for anything. The other three were with her, they'd just joined forces on the road, I gather. There's a strange community feeling among these people, nothing to do with camp-fire jollity or self-congratulatory socialism; something simpler and more tenuous, with no questions asked. They were travelling and living in an old truck that was almost on its last legs, okay for the long hot summer, but an ice box in winter. I'd have put them all up if I'd had a place of my own, but the hotel's too small to get away with even one extra body in your room.'

'You sound expert,' Zeugma interrupted but he ignored her.

'I thought of the office, but the same applied there. Imagine Miss Peat's face! Then it struck me. The research centre. All that lovely space in the fever hospital! And the electricity was still switched on so that I could display its complete charms to visitors. So one dark November evening when all decent folk were in front of the television, I led the way out there, unlocked the gates and set them up. It was just for a few weeks, till the worst of the winter was over. No one was going to want to look over the place till the New Year. In fact from the look of my files, no one seemed keen on looking over it any time in the forseeable future!

'Everything was fine. They had a little bit of cash and I usually did the shopping for them, supplementing their stuff as much as I could afford to. All went smoothly till Sayer decided to do a private tour of inspection. Christ! the bloody row there was! Julie managed to give the impression that somehow they'd found their own way in and said they'd pleaded with me to let them stay there a couple of nights on humanitarian grounds. At least that's what I gathered from Sayer when he came back like an avenging fury, shrieking for my blood. He'd told them to pack up and go, he yelled at me. And he felt like telling me to do the same. I didn't have to say much, he did all the talking. But I felt like telling him to stuff the job and joining Julie and her mates on the road.

'Next day I drove out to the centre to hear their version. But when I got there the place was deserted. They'd gone. I was disappointed, naturally. But I just thought they'd taken Sayer seriously and decided to get out before he turned up with the police. The truck wasn't licensed or insured, I suspect, and they wouldn't want to brush with the law.

'That was in mid-January. Every day I expected some message from Julie. And when nothing came on Valentine's Day, I began to get really concerned.'

'Valentine's Day?' queried Zeugma.

'My birthday. I'd heard from Julie on February 14th every year since I could remember. So I went and saw the police. They were polite, but not very helpful. Hippies rate alongside gypsies as somebody else's problem. But they checked on the vehicle – road accidents, that kind of thing – and assured me nothing was known. Meanwhile I went back up to the centre and had a good look around. I found various items, some clothing, a pair of Julie's shoes, stuff I didn't think she would have wanted to leave. So back to the police I went and that's when the great explosion occurred. Poor Sergeant Fell got most of it, I'm afraid, though he was least at fault. But it was clear that if I was going to get anything done, I'd have to start it myself. Which meant hanging around here, which meant (or so I believed) having access to the research centre . . .'

'. . . which meant keeping your job. So enter Diss of Charnell Bearings,' said Zeugma.

'That's it. God, but it sounds half-witted! But I'm so convinced something must have happened to Julie. Perhaps not the others, they were nothing to me, I would hardly know them again if we met. But Julie . . .'

A light was beginning to dawn in Zeugma's mind.

'This morning you went to see Fell,' she said rapidly. 'And he told you about Crow. Right? About that business with the girl. So you started thinking there might be a connection and that's why you're out here!'

Her face was flushed with excitement beneath the patina of ash. She jumped to her feet.

'Miss Gray, Zeugma,' he began, but there was no time to spare for idle chatter.

'Listen,' she said eagerly, 'that's why I came here today too. Because of the girl. I thought it was that girl in the papers, but it could be your cousin! As well I mean. It would fit. Look, I'm sorry, I'm not explaining things well, but there isn't much time. She was blonde, you say?'

Lakenheath nodded, a look of bewilderment on his face.

'And shoes, what size shoes did she wear? No, you wouldn't know that, would you? But you might recognize . . . hang on a sec.'

She hurried into the far chamber, picked up the shoe and stocking from the shelf and hurried back like a puppy with a stick.

'You see these things? Now, can you remember, think

hard, did your cousin own a pair of shoes like this one? Did she?'

Something of her urgency seemed to have communicated itself to Lakenheath who only took a moment to glance at the shoe before replying. 'Why, yes.'

'And the size? Is that the same? Could this shoe be Julie's?'

'Yes, it could. In fact I'm almost certain it is.'

'Oh my God!' said Zeugma. It was not just Lakenheath's answer that caused the exclamation but a sense of approach, as if some presence was getting nearer to the cottage.

Lakenheath was a big man, but he had an injured ankle and in any case Crow was no weakling. And that dog! With Twinkle at your opponent's throat, you didn't need a size advantage.

'We've got to get out of here!' she assured Lakenheath urgently. 'Come on! The Range Rover's not far.'

'But why . . . ?' he protested.

'Oh come on!' she yelled, trying to drag him to his feet.

But it was too late. Even as the reluctant man began to rise, she heard the strong beat of broad wings, and through the door swept the peregrine. It gave one ear-splitting screech when it saw the intruders, then settled on some hidden perch in the far recesses of the building from which only its eye, gleaming in the daylight which crept through the door, was visible.

Zeugma and Lakenheath held their position in a silent tableau.

Next to arrive was Twinkle, who slid silently across the threshold and lay just inside, making it quite clear that no one was leaving without his permission.

And finally the bulk of a man blotted out the light and Crow stood in the door.

The best thing Zeugma decided was to try to bluff it out. Holding the shoe behind her back, she tried to put on her reassuring Queen Mother smile. But it was instantly apparent that this was in vain.

'Twinkle,' said Crow sternly. 'We have guests.'

Silently the dog rose and, with open jaws and his eyes glistening redly, ran purposefully towards them.

Zeugma abandoned pretence and raised the shoe like a weapon, ready to sell her life dearly.

The dog ignored her and went on to Lakenheath, who stretched out his hand and scratched it between the ears.

'Hello, Twinkle,' he said. 'Hello, Crow.'

'Hello, Sam,' said Crow. 'Shall we have a cup of tea?'

Two shocks in such quick succession proved too much for Zeugma and she sat in a silence which was only partly diplomatic while Crow expertly arranged a handful of twigs in the hearth, lit them, added a couple of solid billets and wedged a kettle on the resultant pyre. Lakenheath regarded her with open amusement on his face and she felt a strong desire to kick him on his strapping. She felt deterred, however, by the presence of Twinkle, who lay at Lakenheath's feet and gave every sign of being a great admirer of the man.

Crow went into the far section and she heard him speak softly to the falcon; at least she hoped it was the falcon; she shuddered at the thought that there might have been other livestock present while she conducted her search. When he returned he bore three mugs and the jug of whisky she had already sampled. This it turned out was used as a substitute for milk in the mug of strong black tea which her host eventually put into her hand.

'So,' he repeated, standing between the two visitors, 'We have guests.'

Zeugma found her voice. It was rather more high-pitched than usual.

'Yes,' she said. 'I thought I'd come and see you about

the money I won from Mr Upas. It struck me that . . .'

Lakenheath choked into his tea and she realized she was going to get no support there.

'And you didn't mind a wait?' Crow said. 'Not even when you saw me running north many miles away? That was kind.'

So much for deception. Did he see *everything*? She decided confrontation was the best policy.

'I'm sorry,' she said. 'No, that wasn't why I came. The reason was to search your house. I noticed this last night,' she held up the shoe, 'and I read the newspaper cutting about the girl.'

'So you came to prove me a murderer,' said Crow. 'Not so kind.'

His voice was stern and she felt her spirits quailing once more. To her surprise. Lakenheath intervened.

'An understandable mistake, Crow,' he said. 'She could have gone squealing to the police.'

He leaned across in front of Crow's body and said. 'Those things you found *are* Julie's. I brought them to Crow myself. He has a way of working things out but he needs a point of contact.'

'Does he? Well he hasn't done much good as far as I can see,' said Zeugma, glancing up at the impassive figure between them. 'And what about my bones, did you take those as well?'

Crow nodded and drank his tea.

'The dead,' he said softly, 'the dead confuse me. Here there are many. So violent, aye, some violent beyond endurance of understanding. And still fresh, always fresh. It does not fade easily, that agony. His in your pit and the man's yesterday in the flames, it is the same agony and I have not always the skill to separate them.'

Zeugma did not understand all this but she felt she had got the gist.

'You mean you took them in case they had something to do with Lakenheath's hippies?'

She snorted derisively with the contempt of the expert.

'When you've done a few digs, you don't need black magic to sort out the old from the new. And why did you keep the hand?'

Crow looked down at her with cold, slate-grey eyes.

'I kept it to bury. One part must remain here where he died no matter what indignities the rest undergoes.'

This reduced Zeugma to silence again and she concentrated on her potent tea.

Now Lakenheath and Crow started talking together and she eavesdropped openly on them. They did not seem to object and when Lakenheath told the other man about Diss and went on to say that the impostor had not put in an appearance that morning, she felt sufficiently bold to interrupt with an account of her meeting at Bewcastle.

'And he warned me against you,' she concluded, nodding at Lakenheath.

'Coals to Bewcastle,' he replied. 'Crow, could this fellow have anything to do with Julie's disappearance, do you think? I got the feeling this morning that Fell knew something about him I didn't.'

Crow shook his head slowly.

'I do not know. I have not felt him yet. There are barriers, all kinds of barriers. Three days ago, I felt close, very close to something. Then it went. Suddenly. It moved away behind a barrier.'

'Moved?' said Lakenheath hopefully. 'You mean she could be alive, on the move?'

'Perhaps, though before I did not think so. Do not hope.'

On that gloomy note, the meeting broke up. They finished their tea, then Lakenheath stood up.

'Thanks, Crow. I'm sorry I won't be able to join you for a while.'

He motioned down at his foot. Crow stared at it for an instant, then reached down and placed his hands on either side of the ankle and pressed firmly. Zeugma flinched and waited for the outcry from Lakenheath but none came.

'Another day,' said Crow, standing up.

Outside the house, Zeugma said to Lakenheath, 'And how are you getting home?'

'With you,' he said cheerfully.

'Really. And if I hadn't been here, how did you propose to get back? In a falcon's beak?'

'No. Crow would have drummed up one of the foresters from somewhere. He's quite matey with them, knows how to talk to the trees. But with you here, it's silly to take them from their work.'

No one ever thinks it's silly to take me from my work, thought Zeugma bitterly.

A few spots of rain began to fall as they reached the Range Rover. Zeugma lifted her face to the sky and felt it on her face. It was gentle and soft compared with the wind-driven violence of the previous day's downpour and it was even possible for the romantic optimist to sense in it the onset of spring. She felt far from romantically optimistic and merely groaned at the thought of her waterlogged trench. But something in her responded to the variegated soft greys of the sky.

'Don't you know enough to get in out of the rain?' asked Lakenheath.

'I was just thinking, what a huge sky,' said Zeugma.

'Were you? That's what Diss said too.'

This brought her out of her reverie and she climbed in beside him and started up.

'Tell me,' she said as they moved away, 'how do you, the concrete-spreader, come to be bosom friends with Crow, the original earth-father?'

'We have things in common,' he said smugly.

'Such as?'

'Well, we run together. I like to keep fit. Shortly after my arrival here, I put on my track suit, drove out into the wilds a bit so that my admirers in Brampton wouldn't get a free laugh, and set off at a gentle jog along the line of the wall, just the other side of Gilsland. Suddenly I had company. Crow and Twinkle. That was how it started.'

'He didn't con you into racing against the dog, did he?'

Lakenheath laughed.

'He tried, but I wasn't having any. I know my limitations. I think that's how it started, when he saw I wasn't an easy mark. After that I ran into him, literally, several times and eventually it became an understood thing. Not that I stick with them all the way. No, you'd need to be Olympic marathon standard for that. You know when he runs, he's not just doing it to keep fit or for kicks. Hell, no!'

'Well, why does he do it?' asked Zeugma.

'I'm not really sure. From what he's said, and what I've observed myself, his runs trace complicated patterns over the waste, too large to be analysed from ground level. There've been archaeological discoveries of such things, haven't there? Formal patterns too huge to be discerned except from the air?'

'Yes, there have,' said Zeugma. 'Space-ship landing sites, some fools believe. But you mean Crow's doing something like outlining a huge pentacle to work his charms in? That's dafter still!'

'Perhaps. I was curious enough to try to check on the pattern. One of my little schemes to try to keep poor Sayer and his lads happy was to have the whole area photographed from the air. Good selling point to prospective developers, I claimed. And I thought that perhaps Crow might have been trotting round the place long enough to leave a track! But, hell, when they came through a few weeks ago, I found it was like trying to read Greek when you'd opted for German at school!'

'Yes, they can be confusing,' said Zeugma.

He glanced at her with a grin and she realized that she'd sounded rather pedagogically superior.

'You're welcome to a look,' he said. 'Anyway, to continue about Crow, he proved very helpful when Julie and the others were here. Often left a rabbit or a couple of birds at the centre gate.'

'He knew they were there then?' said Zeugma thoughtfully.

'Of course. There's not much goes on round here without it coming to Crow's notice eventually. So when I started to worry about Julie and got nowhere with the police, I went to Crow and asked him to help.'

'It's like going to the local witch-doctor,' scoffed Zeugma. 'You don't believe in all this supernatural stuff, do you?'

'You've got to believe in something,' said Lakenheath surprisingly. 'Crow's different, that I'm sure of. Though how he's different I don't know. What I do know is that when he found that other girl, she was buried five feet down in an old stream bed beneath half a dozen layers of stones. You need something special to do that.'

'Like knowing where to look,' said Zeugma, but she gunned the engine as she did so and they bumped over a rise and started running down to the centre road below.

'Do you mind going up to the centre before we make for Brampton?' asked Lakenheath.

Cheeky sod, thought Zeugma, but she turned obediently when they reached the road and drove towards the formidable gates.

They sat in silence for a while, staring out into the gently falling rain like a family party on a day's outing to almost any English seaside resort almost any day in summer.

'What strikes me about it,' said Zeugma finally, 'is that it's so small. I mean, it's a jolly sight too big for here, in this particular place, but it doesn't look as if much could have gone on there really. And why did they need to shut off so much of the surrounding countryside? I know it's down now, but according to Charley, there used to be a ring of wire and warning notices about five miles in diameter.'

'There's a lot underground,' said Lakenheath. 'Several of the labs. And the test chamber too. And last, but not least, the fuel-storage chambers. Now there were four of those, all on the left hand side of the square, which is where the test chamber was. They staggered them for safety; the first starts about twenty yards out of the perimeter line, the next forty and so on.'

'What do you mean, for safety?'

He grinned happily, his turn to be schoolmaster.

'Don't you know anything about rocket fuels?' he asked scornfully.

'No,' Zeugma replied.

'Thank God for that. Neither do I. But I gather that the stuff they've had down there ranging from ethyl alcohol to fluorine with a soupçon of liquid hydrogen and perhaps a dash of diborane could have lifted most of this terrain fifty feet in the air and flipped it over like a pancake. So you see why they had the warning notices spread so wide.'

'It's monstrous, monstrous!' said Zeugma. 'Thank God they've gone and taken their bloody fuel with them.'

'Well, not quite,' said Lakenheath.

'What do you mean? There's some left here?'

She made as if to start the car and drive away. He took her hand and held it from the ignition.

'No, not that. But you've probably been warned sometime that even when a petrol can has been emptied and washed out, it can hold sufficient fumes to flash off if you drop a match in it? Well, these silos are just the same. But never fear. They blocked them off when they pulled out. Took out the pipelines and put concrete plugs in the holes. Couldn't risk a distillery taking over the place and using the tanks as whisky vats! It'd be potent stuff, mind you. Like Crow's! So no danger. All right?'

'Thanks for the reassurance,' said Zeugma. 'But I still

115

find it a creepy place. Are we going to sit here all day, just staring?'

'What? Sorry. No, let's go now by all means. I was just thinking about the centre. It really is the *centre*, isn't it? That's where whatever happened to Julie happened, I'm sure of that. You know, they, Julie and her mates, used to say the place was haunted, bumps in the night, that sort of thing.'

'Just Crow's cup of tea,' commented Zeugma, starting the car.

'Then something else struck me. Diss. He never gave me the keys back. He locked the gates behind him when he left the centre. Later after Sayer's accident, it never occurred to me to ask for them back.'

'Why on earth should he want the keys to that place?' asked Zeugma.

'Search me. Fortunately there's a duplicate set in the office. Now I wonder, I wonder.'

He looked calculatingly at Zeugma, who thought, He's going to ask me to do something else for him.

'Doing anything special tonight?' he asked casually.

'Yes,' she replied with great emphasis. 'I have a dinner engagement. In Liddesdale.'

'Ah. Upas. The young hero. Give him my regards. Look,' he said, 'what I was going to ask you was this. I've got a feeling it might be worth our while to keep an eye on the centre . . .'

'Worth *our* while!' she interrupted. 'Where does that *our* come from?'

'Well, you did break into Crow's house because you were worried about a crime, didn't you?' he said almost apologetically. 'No, what I meant was, a kind of vigil, just a couple of nights . . .'

Again she interrupted.

'You want me to spend a night in that place with you? You're crazy!'

'Perhaps,' he said. 'No, I don't want you to stay there

with me. What I would appreciate, though, is if you could find time to drop me there this evening before you go to dinner and pick me up when you come back.'

He said it as if it was the smallest thing in the world, a diversion of a hundred yards or so.

'What a cheek!' she exclaimed. 'It's miles out of my way! I'd have to come into Brampton to pick you up, then drive you out . . . no! I won't think of it. Drive yourself. You've had the healing hands touch. Just test it out. Or get a taxi. It's a crazy idea. I don't want anything to do with it.'

But I will, she thought gloomily. I will. Years of Whitethorn experience had taught her that there was no method of stopping the elegant, the good-looking, the self-confident from getting their own way.

The rest of the journey was passed in silence. When they reached Brampton, he asked her to take him to his office in Front Street. She would then have driven straight off, but he staggered badly as he got out of the car and asked if she could help him up the stairs.

Sighing, she brought up the rear, ready to catch him if he fell.

Miss Peat sat in her corner, only her eyes moving as they entered. She looked as if she had not left her seat since last Zeugma saw her. Perhaps the cleaner just dusted round her.

Lakenheath greeted her cheerfully. Miss Peat had not been the most lively companion he had ever sat drinking with, but the ease with which she dispatched glass after glass of Pernod had given her a new human dimension. And she had been the perfect listener.

'You might as well see those pics while you're here,' said Lakenheath to Zeugma. 'Then we can chat about tonight's arrangements.'

'Oh no,' she said, following him into his office.

He dug into his desk drawers and triumphantly emerged with a large buff envelope from which he spilled a couple of dozen aerial photographs.

'Take a look at those,' he said. 'Let's hear what the experts make of them.'

Her reaction surprised him. She seized the photographs from the table and thumbed through them with all the avid curiosity of a schoolboy with his first nudist magazine.

'Is anything the matter?' he asked.

'Oh, no. No. They're very good, aren't they? And you had them done specially for the Development Council?'

'Right. You archaeologists want any of them, you buy the copyright from me.'

Zeugma smiled faintly. But as she did so she wondered in some bewilderment how copies of these same photographs taken so recently had come so soon into the hands of Dr Leo Pasquino.

11

'Tis opportune to look back upon old times. We have enough to do to make up ourselves from present and passed times, and the whole stage of things scarce serveth for our instruction.

Lakenheath must have been watching from the foyer of the hotel, for he came limping out of the front door just as she arrived.

'You look as if you're going to the office on the seven-twenty-five,' she said, nodding at the ancient briefcase he was carrying.

'Do I? It's just a little light refreshment in case I get peckish. And some reading matter.'

'How disappointing. I made sure you'd have an old service revolver at least,' she said primly setting the Range Rover in motion.

'No. Sorry. The service I did never reached the revolver-owning stage.'

'Ah!' she said. 'You told me you were never in the army.'

'No. I said I was never an officer in a fashionable regiment,' he said. 'But I *was* a boy soldier.'

'What?'

'Yes! Signed on the dotted line when I was fifteen. I wanted out of that terrible school and I didn't want in to the kind of job lads like myself were getting just then.'

'Ah. The deprived child syndrome,' she said, then flushed hideously and unconcealably as she felt his cool gaze rest on her profile.

'Could be,' he said, and fell silent.

'What happened?' she asked. To finish there would leave her very much in the wrong.

'Oh, I stuck it for four, five years,' he said. 'Passed some exams I wouldn't have got if I'd stayed at school. Saw a bit of the world before it ended. My army career, I mean!'

'And how did it end?' she asked.

'Fortuitously,' he said. 'By the time I was nineteen, I'd had enough. Unfortunately I'd signed on for twelve years.'

'So what happened?'

'Like I said, fortuitously about this time the army decided to dispense with my services.'

'Oh. I see.'

She didn't see at all. The first picture that came into her mind was of Lakenheath getting the sack for turning up late on parade three mornings in a row, but surely even the modern army did not work like that? The second picture was of Lakenheath having all his badges of rank stripped from him on the open square while a muffled drum beat insistently in the background. But that was officers only, wasn't it?

And for the third picture she had to turn to her memories of the girl at Whitethorn who was so expert on the Turkish Army Officers' Manual. She had a brother seven years older than herself who she claimed had avoided National Service by faking *both* the only two fool-proof methods of making yourself unwanted by the army.

These were bed-wetting and homosexuality.

She risked a sideways glance at Lakenheath and tried to see him as either enuretic or queer.

Perhaps his subsequent career would give a clue.

'What did you do then?' she asked.

'After the army? Well, I felt like a rest, something completely different. So I gathered up my little certificate, trotted round to my local education office and managed to get myself accepted at a teachers' training college.'

She greeted this with even more incredulity than she had done the revelation of his army background.

'You – a teacher?'

'You – an archaeologist?' he replied. 'I lasted out my three-year course, though it wasn't as much different from the army as I'd hoped; then I did my probationary year, just to get the service in. After that I went on a bit of a walkabout for eighteen months.'

'Some walk!'

'It was. I did the length of Britain to start with, not walking all the time, mind you. In fact, I started off with Julie and some of her mates, but they were too purposeless for me. I ended up in the Shetlands, worked my way across to Norway on a trawler, then trotted down Europe till I reached the Med. I got a bit ill in North Africa, so decided it was time I headed home. Back here I got a job in a technical college; I quite liked that and stayed on a couple of years. Then, the tech college got swallowed up in a bigger beast called a College of Advanced Technology which began to have university pretensions, and they started a Business Diploma Course. So I stopped being a teacher and became a student again.'

'So you *were* at a university,' she accused.

'I suppose so. But not much like Oxford and Cambridge, I reckon! We worked hard. I got through, thought it was silly to waste my new-found abilities in the classroom and got a very junior job with a consultancy firm in the Midlands. Now that was really dull, but really. It was all words, you see. There was nothing concrete there, or if there was, then I didn't get a sniff at it. A layer of groundbait, that's all I was. So I wanted out after a year, saw this job advertised, applied never imagining that anyone as inexperienced as me would even be interviewed, and, lo and behold! here I am!'

'Applause, applause,' she said. 'They saw through the veneer to the sterling qualities beneath.'

'Well,' he said cheerfully, 'they were dead wrong, weren't they?'

Zeugma now glanced at the clock in the dashboard and pursed her lips. She would need to get a move on if she were to get back to the Old Kith in time for Upas. Though it might do that young man good to be kept waiting. His recent heroics had probably confirmed his beliefs in his own irresistibility.

No! she told herself. I must get out of this awful middle-aged habit of deciding I know what might do other people good.

It was a dark, dark night, there was no star-light, and their only contact with the outside world was the swish of the rain from beneath the tyres and the cones of light the Range Rover pushed before it.

Suddenly the thought of dropping Lakenheath in these conditions in the middle of nowhere to sit and wait for God-knows-what was intolerable.

'This is absurd,' she said.

'What is?'

'You can't go and sit in that place all by yourself all night. I don't know how late I may be. The thought of you will spoil my dinner.'

'Oh good. I thought for one moment a touch of the altruistics had crept in. Never fear. I'll be fine.'

'What about Diss?'

'Diss-appeared,' he laughed. 'I checked at his hotel and he's cleared out of there. No one seems to have seen him since you had your little chat yesterday. Perhaps he's crept away with his tail between his legs.'

The mockery was gentle, but she was as ready to be

exasperated as those whose unselfish solicitude is rejected usually are.

'Well, I suppose you can come to no harm then,' she snapped.

'Just what I've been trying to say,' he said, with the calm self-assurance of one who has won an argument beyond all doubt.

They didn't speak again till they reached the centre. Lakenheath hopped out and unlocked the gates.

'I'll drive you up to the hospital,' she offered. It was only forty or fifty yards but at Lakenheath's rate of progress he would be soaked by the time he got there.

'No thanks,' he said. 'I'll have to lock the gate on the inside, otherwise it's a bit obvious someone's here.'

'Of course,' she said. 'What shall I do when I come to pick you up?'

He thought for a second.

'Just blow your horn. Three blasts. Morse for S.'

'And what does S stand for?' she asked.

He grinned.

'Whatever you like. Thanks for the lift. See you later.'

The gates crashed shut, she heard the key in the lock and then Lakenheath's footsteps moving towards the hospital which, near though it was, was almost invisible in the sodden darkness.

She reversed and headed back along the road. By day she would have followed one of the moorland routes which had now become so familiar to her. But in these conditions with visibility so poor and the atmosphere of the deserted centre still touching her mind, she vowed nothing on God's earth would get her driving across the waste that night. Nothing.

Upas was sitting at the bar talking to Charley when she entered the Old Kith.

'At last,' he said. 'But well worth the waiting.'

He stood up, took her hand and gave it a kiss which got very close to being a bite, an impression confirmed

123

by the way he pursed his lips reflectively afterwards as though sampling a new foodstuff, then he said softly, '. . . tasting of Flora and the country green, dance and Provençal song, and sunburnt mirth.'

Why do they all get around to Keats in the end? she wondered resignedly. All that vigorous sensuousness. If only someone would quote a Cavalier lyric at me. Or, better still, something elegant and polished and *fleshless* from the middle of the eighteenth century. Still, it was better than nothing, which was what she had got from Lakenheath.

'Shall we go, or would you like another drink?' she asked.

'I think not.'

'Oh. Black heart needs a clear head, is that it? Well, good-night, Charley. This, by the way, is Mr Upas.'

'We've met,' said Charley. 'Drive carefully, sir. Lot of stray dogs round here. I'd hate for you to get close to one!'

Zeugma glared at him, angry at his rudeness, but Upas laughed out loud.

'Someone's been talking, I see. Well, there's always a second time.'

'Not for paying debts, there isn't,' said Zeugma. 'Ten pounds, remember?'

He looked at her quizzically, then reached inside the lose suède jerkin he had substituted for the riding leathers and produced a roll of notes.

'I like to start even,' he said, peeling off two fivers and passing them over.

'Thanks, she said. 'Let's go, then.'

She expected to see a car outside. Instead there was just the motor-bike.

'You've come on that?' she said.

'Yes. Climb aboard.'

'No thanks,' she said firmly.

'No? Why not?'

'First I've no intention of getting wet. Second, you

may not have noticed but I'm wearing a skirt. I am not going to roll it up round my waist and be a free show for everyone we meet. Nor am I going to risk my neck by sitting on the pillion side-saddle. I'll bring the Range Rover. You lead, I'll follow.'

He didn't argue, and a couple of minutes later they set off into the night.

The temperature had risen as the wind dropped that day, but it was still chilly and as they climbed out of the relatively protected valley in which Blackrigg lay, Zeugma felt glad for reasons other than safety and modesty that she'd rejected the bike. She'd no desire to arrive at her host's house with her flesh corrugated with goose pimples and her hair like a rook's nest.

Also travelling like this meant that there would be no need for anyone to accompany her back to the pub and she would be able to go direct to the centre to collect Lakenheath. In addition (a less positive advantage perhaps) there would be no opportunity for good-night grapples and muffled mutterings about warm, white, lucent, million-pleasured breasts. Though she might be doing Upas an injustice of course. Why should an attractive, self-confident young swinger like that have designs on such as she? If he'd been after her lily-white body, surely he'd have left his bike at the Old Kith and accompanied her in the Rover, thus ensuring that he made the return trip with her?

Her elation ebbed. It was one thing to have foiled the lecherous plans of a personable young man. It was quite another for there to have been no such plans in the first place.

She resolutely checked this drift of her thoughts, partly on the grounds of self-esteem and partly because it would be far too easy just to follow Upas's bike blindly and be left with no idea of the route home.

It was still very dark and it was difficult to pick out the young man's shape. The tail-light ahead bounced and swayed like a disembodied will-o'-the-wisp and she began to fantasize about being led over moor and fen, through bog and briar to some strange unearthly fate. She had worked too many times in remote and lonely places not to have felt that there were appetites in nature which the mere animal kingdom could not understand; her scepticism in the face of people like Crow was nine-tenths self-reassurance in the face of deep-planted fears.

She snapped the headlights full on and the metalled road and the motor-bike shook their heads reprovingly at her absurdity, saying:

'We are made by man, we are your servants, trust us and follow.'

Half an hour later, without having met another vehicle on the road, she followed Upas through a gateway between two huge holly bushes and along a curving rough stone drive for a distance of some half a mile. Trees and shrubs huddled close on either side, principally gnarled and postulated beeches in a regular colonade crammed between with blackthorn and mountain ash whose red berries gleamed in the headlights like drops of blood.

Then they rounded the final bend and ahead lay the house. It was just a dark rectangle at first, almost invisible against the hills which rose up beyond it. Only one light could be seen and that was the fitful glow of a fire-lit room on the first floor. But when Upas came to a dramatic halt with whatever was the equivalent in motorcycling of a parallel stop Christiania, lights burgeoned all over the house and before Zeugma had brought the Range Rover to a standstill, the front door had opened, laying a carpet of light invitingly out of the stone porchway on to the drive.

A figure moved into the porch, and came to a halt silhouetted against the doorway, tall and thin; for a moment Zeugma thought it was Pasquino, then smiled ruefully as she climbed out of the Range Rover and saw it was a woman.

Her hair was cut close to the contours of her skull, producing an Egyptian Nefertiti effect, and indeed there was something Arabic about the structure of her face. Her skin was pale but with the ineradicable sallowness which derives from generations of familiarity with an uncompromising sun. She stood almost six foot tall and incredibly thin, the black shirt and slacks she wore giving the merest hint of feminine roundness of breast or buttock. Her eyes were huge and brown almost to blackness and around the narrow wrist of her long left arm she wore seven gold bangles which clinked together with a rich dullness as she now moved forward and extended both hands to Zeugma in greeting.

In the woman, the gesture appeared both graceful and natural, but Zeugma (quickly deciding it would be boorishly stuffy to reply with the conventional Whitethorn firm handshake) felt absurdly histrionic as she reached out her own short well-fleshed arms in reply and allowed the woman to grasp them. Her fingers were smooth and cold. They momentarily explored the work-roughened surfaces of Zeugma's skin, then turned the hands round so she could look at the palms.

Now she smiled and said something in a foreign language, adding almost immediately, 'Forgive me. I say you are welcome to this house.'

Her voice was surprisingly rich and deep.

'Thank you,' said Zeugma. 'I am pleased to be here.'

But her recent stay in Egypt had left her with more than a smattering of the language and she was trying to recall a welcome idiom in Arabic which said *this cow will live for ever.*

She withdrew her hands gently but firmly and looked at Upas enquiringly.

'I'm being remiss,' he said with a grin. 'You two haven't been introduced and clearly in Britain nothing can go any further till this is seen too. My love, this is Miss Gray. Zeugma, this is Amine. My sister.'

'How do you do?' said Zeugma.

'Welcome,' said Amine. 'I am sorry to have to start your evening with a disappointment.'

'Disappointment?' echoed Zeugma.

'Yes,' said Amine, leading her into the house. 'I'm afraid that dear Leo will not, after all, be dining with us this evening.'

'What?' Zeugma found it was quite beyond her to conceal the depth of her disappointment.

'Yes, I know. It is a blow,' said Amine sympathetically.

'But why?'

'It is idiotic. Today he and a friend of ours borrowed one of our cars and drove up into the Lothians. Leo had expressed a wish to look at the henge and cairn at Cairn-papple Hill. Do you know it? Unfortunately their car has broken down. They just telephoned half an hour ago. In this part of the world, repairs are difficult enough in working hours, at night almost impossible. Fortunately there is an inn close by where they can stay till morning.'

Zeugma could have wept with disappointment.

'They can't be all that far,' she protested. 'Couldn't someone fetch them? I don't mind going in the Range Rover.'

She made a movement towards the vehicle, but the long cool fingers took her hand once more.

'No. They are quite far. Fifty, sixty miles perhaps. Almost two hours on these roads in the dark. Perhaps you can stay the night and see Leo tomorrow? But come in here now. After the disappointment I have a surprise. Someone I think you know.'

She opened a door and ushered Zeugma into a long drawing room furnished with rather shabby though still elegant Regency pieces. Sitting in a Herculanium arm-chair with his back to them was a man.

'Miss Gray,' said Amine. 'May I present to you my brother Malcolm.'

The man rose at the sound of her voice and turned.

'Hello, Zeugma,' he said.

And suddenly the sense of familiarity she had felt on meeting Jonathan Upas was explained.

The man being introduced to her now as Malcolm Upas had five years earlier been known to her as Hasan bin Radhauri, her friend and lover.

12

Than the time of these Urnes deposited,
or precise Antiquity of these Reliques,
nothing of more uncertainty.

Lakenheath found himself whistling nervously as he settled down to his self-imposed vigil. He had chosen the former staff sitting room as his base in the centre, partly
because it ran the whole breadth of the old fever hospital
and thus had windows overlooking three sides of the quadrangle, and partly because there remained here three or
four old easy chairs which the Ministry had not felt were
worth carting back with the rest of the equipment.

In this room the scientists and administrative staff had
been able to gather for coffee or tea, or a mid-afternoon
nap if the pressures got too strong. Here also Julie and
her friends had set up house during their stay in the
centre. It was here that he had found the bits and pieces
they had left behind which had given him so much concern.

He thought about Julie and their relationship. In many
ways they were totally different. In himself he recognized
the desire for change, for new purposes. Julie, on the other
hand had wanted nothing, or nothing that society could
give her. Her concern was not with the purposes of life,
but with living. He had tried her way for a while, but it
had left him unsatisfied. Even in his wanderings he had
to have a destination.

But they had been close, fitting together like parts of each other, which made sense of their differences. It had nothing to do with physical attraction. They had made love a couple of times, as it seemed a kind of closeness it would be foolish not to try, but it had not added anything to their relationship. That was simple, natural, containing nothing of demands or desires.

And it was too simple, too natural for Lakenheath not to know, despite the hope he had expressed to Crow, that Julie was dead.

It would have been easy to cry. Instead he opened his briefcase, took out and placed in his pocket a large rubber-covered torch, then unearthed a vacuum flask from which he poured himself a cup of coffee, and settled down to wait.

Two hours later his flask was empty and he was still waiting; but for what he grew less and less sure. Like the man jumping into the cactus bush, it had seemed like a good idea at the time. Whatever had happened to Julie had happened here, or close by – of that he was sure. But Sergeant Fell, exasperated by his insistence, had gone over the whole establishment thoroughly without finding anything significant. Of course, Fell's attitude had been that he did not expect to find anything which would predispose the search to failure, but Lakenheath knew him as a hard-working and conscientious officer who would do his job honestly. It had been the curious business of Diss that had refocussed his attention here. He smiled as he recalled his shock when this creature of his own imagination had actually appeared. It had seemed the clever thing to observe rather than confront, particularly with Sayer around.

And now Sayer was no longer around.

He reached into his briefcase again and pulled out a flat half of Scotch. The chill was really getting to him now and he took a long pull even though he had promised himself moderation. He had no desire to anaesthetize himself to whatever mysteries this place might hold.

Though perhaps it would not be a bad idea, he thought, looking round the room. This place must hold mysteries other than his own. His eyes had become quite accustomed to the darkness now, but it was still very easy to imagine this room lined with truckle beds on which lay the twisting bodies of fever-racked patients who perhaps in their own delirium had seen the slow moving emaciated figures of that old farmer and his wife as they crawled from one snow-packed window to another, no longer believing that rescuers would ever come.

He found he was whistling again. Diss, now. Concentrate on Diss. No ghost he, though no less puzzling and frightening for that. Perhaps more so. Substance-less fingers of the spirit world could not press down on shotgun triggers.

He must, surmised Lakenheath, have gone through the files in the office, come across the Charnell Bearings file (not difficult; there was precious little else to come across) and decided to assume that identity.

But why?

If he had come along saying he was the development manager of I.C.I., he would have been welcomed with open arms and undergone far less immediate risk of discovery. In addition, there was the mystery of his revelation of another identity to the police. Fell had thanked him politely when he had put the facts of the case in his hands that morning, but had not indicated what action he would take, if indeed any law had been broken.

Absently, Lakenheath took another swig at the whisky. Its warming effects were local and short-lived, he found. Carefully he rose to his feet and limped round the room, blowing into his hands. The luminous dial of his watch told him that Zeugma was probably in the middle of her dinner. He imagined the warm room, the polished table, the steaming tureen, the bottles of wine and sighed in envy. Perhaps it wasn't like that. Perhaps Upas would only run to a fish supper. Perhaps...

He heard a noise and froze.

It was a metallic scraping noise which for a moment seemed to fill the room.

Slowly, with great self-discipline, he sank down to the floor so that from no angle would his body be outlined against the windows. His ear tried desperately to get a fix on the noise but it was impossible.

He moved his gaze slowly over the room, then rapidly from side to side, hoping to catch any intrusive movement on the off-centre sensitive spot in the retina. But whatever had made the noise was as still as he was. Stiller, for he found that his crouch placed too much strain on his damaged ankle and he had to adjust his position. As he shifted the noise came again and he overbalanced, collapsing noisily to the bare boards. If whatever was in the room with him purposed any physical attack, now was the time. The noise again. He rolled towards it, his mind telling his body to do the unexpected. And again the noise, clearly audible through his own raucous breathing.

This time he pinpointed it.

It came from the radiator.

Slowly he rose, dragging from his pocket the torch. Fortunately its rubber casing had saved it from any damage and the powerful beam stabbed through the darkness like the blade of a friend.

There was nothing there, only a radiator. And then he heard the sound a fifth time.

Someone, somewhere in the centre was doing something to a radiator pipe and the noise was being carried all round the system.

He returned to his briefcase and took from the document pouch a folded sheet of paper which he spread on the floor. It was a plan of the Thirlsike Centre. Being chief officer of N.E.C.D.C. had some advantages. It confirmed what his memory had told him, that the central heating system took in the whole of the complex, not just the hospital. This meant the source of the noise could be in any one of more than twenty rooms. For a second Lakenheath contemplated hammering his heavy-duty working boot against the radiator and giving whoever was at the other end a taste of his own terror. But it would have been a stupid gesture, sacrificing his main advantage, which was surprise. He took one last look at his map and then set out on his tour of exploration.

The hospital was linked to the quadrangle buildings by two covered ways. Lakenheath left by the one nearest the staff sitting room. He moved slowly, with the caution both of the stalker and the invalid. His ankle injury was much improved, but he felt that before the night was out he might find himself needing to use his feet as though nothing had happened and till then it was worth conserving his strength.

The covered way was glass-sided from waist-level up, so he crouched low to make as little silhouette as he could. The feel of the heavy-headed stick in his hand was a comfort to him.

In his other hand he carried a bunch of three keys. Every room in the centre could be opened by one or the other of these masters but to his surprise he didn't need his keys for the first door. A rule of the place since the 'hippie invasion' (Sayer's term) had been that after any tour of the centre with a development client, *all* doors, internal and external, must be locked. Sayer and Diss had been the last visitors. Officially.

He thought once more of Sayer's death. When he had talked with Fell about Diss earlier that day, he had asked about the accident. The blow-out theory was repeated, but he was not convinced. That old car couldn't have been going fast enough to pose such difficulties of control.

Sayer was a good driver, used to driving his own three-and-a-half-litre Rover. A heart attack, perhaps? There had to be a first time.

He put the puzzle out of his mind and carefully tried the first laboratory door. This too was unlocked. He pushed it gently open and entered on all fours. It was uncomfortable and undignified, but the nearest he could manage to the shoulder-charge followed by the flying dive and somersault so favoured by cops and cowboys on the telly screen.

He knew the centre well, knew that this lab, like the others, had been stripped of everything re-usuable and was now merely a litter-strewn barn, but the feeling of vast emptiness he experienced now came as a surprise. At least it was emptiness he felt, he told himself. The radiator sound came again, making him start, but also reassuring him. It sounded fainter here, as though he had moved further from its source, or else the source itself was becoming weaker. Now he felt able to switch on the torch and send its beam prying into the darkness.

Instantly the room assumed its proper proportions. It was quite empty.

He returned to the corridor and made his way to the next door. This he knew led down a flight of steps into the concrete bunker which ran the full length of this side of the quadrangle and off which the four main storage tanks were situated at staggered distances. He felt a vague disinclination to descend beneath ground level. The darkness was bad enough when you knew that the sky and open air were yours at the opening of a window; but the bunker was too tomb-like for his present state of nerves.

Besides, the radiator system did not penetrate down there, so it was not an area which concerned his present investigation.

Relieved, though feeling slightly Jesuitical, he passed on.

Fifteen minutes later he had reached the gatehouse

and met with no success. The sound continued and had begun to fall very sinisterly on his ears, less like something scraping against a radiator pipe and more like a chain being dragged across a stone floor, or sometimes a slab being shifted from a sarcophagus.

Neither of which sounds I have ever heard, he told himself sensibly. But it was a relief to step out of the gatehouse and stand in the cool night air for a few moments before crossing behind the gate and resuming his search on the other side.

He paused a while at the gate itself, peering through the close-set bars. The damp road reflected what little light there was and its faint luminescence hypnotized his eyes and his heart. It led to habitations, to people, to lights. It led to the hotel bar, the friendly greeting, the hand going uninstructed to the whisky bottle. It might even lead to the Scottish chambermaid with the cruel teeth and the wanton walk.

He glanced at his watch and groaned. There were hours yet before he could hope to leave this place. At the very earliest, he couldn't expect the girl to get here before midnight. And from the look of her she was a good trencher-woman and it might be a damn sight later than that.

There was nothing for it but to carry on.

Re-entering the rectangle of buildings was like crawling back down a tunnel from which you have just escaped. Each successive empty room brought a mixture of relief and increased foreboding. He had not yet had to use his keys. All doors were unlocked.

Which means, he reassured himself jocularly, that at least I am dealing with a human agent.

Something scuttered down the corridor behind him and he whirled round, switching on the torch. Nothing. The vacant beam revealed nothing. Dust and a few dried leaves which some previous visit had permitted to be blown in.

Leaves blowing in the wind terrifying me, he thought. This is yet another job I find I'm not the man for. Frightened of dead leaves?

But what causes the wind that blows the leaves?

He found the answer in the next room. He halted outside as he realized the door was ajar. Hanging from it by a single screw was a nameplate which read *Dr Albert Healot*. It swung gently as he pushed at the door and the image rose in his mind of Healot himself, choking at the end of the rope he used to end his life.

But that had been many miles from here. This room could hold no ghosts.

Instead it held chaos. The floor was torn up, the walls had huge pits gouged out of them, even the ceiling had been torn away to reveal the metal cross-beams. It was as if some pickaxe-wielding poltergeist had conceived a deep and bitter hatred for this place.

This was where the leaf-scattering draught had come from. Two of the large window-panes were shattered and the frame itself sagged to one side as a result of the violent assault on the wall.

Lakenheath surveyed the mess in bewilderment. Aimless, savage vandalism in urban areas was accepted almost without comment, but who would come to this lonely place just to destroy a single room?

It looked fairly recent. Indeed it *must* be fairly recent.

Had it been done before Sayer and Diss made their visit? Or even during the visit? That was an interesting thought, but one on which he could build no viable hypothesis.

He switched off the torch and resumed his tour.

Twenty minutes later he had been round the full square and, apart from Healot's room, found nothing. The noise had continued, however, and once more he sat down on the floor and examined his plan. There had to be a solution which did not admit of supernatural agencies.

If, he said to himself, if there is a noise being transmitted via the radiator pipes, and if I have been in every room in the centre which contains a radiator, then the noise must originate ... where?

The answer was ludicrously simple.

From the actual starting-point of the pipes. The boiler-room itself!

He rapped his foot angrily with his stick and yelled with pain. This was where he should have started. The trouble was, the plan included neither the bunkers beneath the quadrangle buildings nor the basement of the hospital. And it was in the latter that the boiler house was situated.

Back to square one, he thought, as he trudged wearily along the covered walk once more. He made no attempt at concealment this time. If there were anyone or anything alert and watching in the centre, he must have been spotted long before this. In addition his ankle was throbbing distress signals, he was very cold and he was beginning to feel very ill-tempered.

He let the anger build up, though one part of his mind was able to see objectively that what he was really doing was finding a substitute for his ebbing courage. The wear and tear on the nerves of his solitary vigil had been greater than he had foreseen, and to tiptoe stealthily down the basement stairs now seemed mentally as well as physically impossible.

It was also rendered pointless by what he discovered when he reached the large oaken door which led into the stairs. It was locked, the first locked door he had encountered in his perabulations round the centre.

It was of course the third key he tried which opened it, and there was no question of turning keys deftly in the oiled wards; they rattled, the lock made protesting clicking noises and the door screeched grimly on rusty hinges.

Below all was dark and silence. If anything lived down there, it lay still and waiting.

Slowly Lakenheath descended the stairs. The torch was

switched on, but its beam which before had seemed so strong and broad now shone feebly and narrowly. How much this was purely subjective, Lakenheath was in no position to assess. His heart was beating fast and he had to swallow hard two or three times to ease the constriction of his throat before he reached the foot of the stairs and turned into the boiler room itself.

The narrow finger of light slowly traced the room's outline, finally resting against the broad cylinder of the flue which ascended from the central-heating boiler. Slowly it ran down the dull metal tube till it lighted on the bulk of the boiler itself, a huge installation to deal with the heating needs of such an establishment. Square and squat it sat, menacing, like all dead machines. The finger sought and found the radiator pipe which set off here on its long journey round the centre. It began to follow its course towards the damp, unplastered wall. But the smooth line of the pipe was broken after only eighteen inches. Something was wrapped round it. Something . . . a joint-lug? a piece of lagging?

A pair of hands.

For a second which seemed much much longer, Lakenheath thought the hands clasped together round the cold metal pipe were disembodied. Just hands. Nothing more. Then in the shadows beyond the pipe he saw a darker shadow. Arms, stretched almost parallel to the pipe. And whoever lay so was concealed by the bulk of the boiler.

'Who's there?' demanded Lakenheath.

There was a grim non-human noise, the hands moved, thin fingers stretched out, there was a rattling of a chain.

Forgetting his ankle, he moved swiftly round the boiler, stick upraised. The figure that lay there turned towards him. At least he assumed it did though it was difficult to say for its head was enclosed in a featureless black hood.

'Who are you?' demanded Lakenheath, and when no answer came, he reached forward, seized the hood and dragged it free. And he staggered back from what he saw.

A face twisted and distorted, a mouth gaping open in a rictus of pain with sounds squeezing their way out between bloodless lips as though the tongue had been ripped from the throat.

He dropped the torch, almost deliberately. Darkness was better than this. And oblivion would be best of all.

'It is quite simple really,' said Malcolm Upas. 'In Britain I am my father's child, in North Africa my mother's. What complications having two names saves!'

He smiled and Zeugma found herself responding easily, willingly to the smile. Five years had not changed him a great deal, she thought. His face was a little fuller, that was all.

'You never told me about Jonathan and Amine,' she said reproachfully.

'I think I did,' he answered. 'But they were still very young five years ago. Sixteen, fifteen. Children. Our talk, I recollect, was of more adult things.'

He glanced at her questioningly. For all his self-assurance, he is uncertain of our relationship now, thought Zeugma.

Jonathan and Amine had discreetly retired almost immediately, and for a couple of minutes thereafter Zeugma had found herself stuttering and stammering in a most un-Whitethornish way. But now she was in control once more and things were beginning to fall into place. As the controller of Leo's correspondence for seven years, it had puzzled her slightly that she had lacked all knowledge of the Upases, friends close enough to whisk him away in the middle of a dig. But now the Upases' double identity was revealed, it left her with another puzzle.

'Why didn't you come back with Leo as soon as you met him?' she asked forthrightly. 'Instead of leaving me to toil – and worry – all by myself?'

Malcolm chose his words carefully.

'I wanted to, of course. But Leo did not mention that you were with him straightaway. And he seemed – how shall I say it? – concerned that no offence should be done to your feelings. I am his friend, but I do not think he approved of our old relationship. He is very protective, dear Leo!'

He ended with a laugh in an attempt to lighten the situation.

'I suppose he is,' agreed Zeugma, thinking, Yes, it figured. Leo might be delighted to meet Hasan again, but be less than pleased at the thought of what effect his sudden reappearance might have on his ward. No doubt there had been some fairly free-speaking during the past couple of days before he had consented to the dinner invitation being transmitted.

Zeugma felt both flattered and offended by these efforts to protect her. She was, after all, a grown woman, and in any case her feelings for Hasan had long since been tucked away among her other bitter-sweet souvenirs. So she re-assured herself, though his presence here was the most unsettling thing she had experienced in these days of unsettling experiences.

'Was it because of anything Leo did or said that you went away in Cairo?' she asked.

'You haven't change, I'm pleased to see,' he said. 'Direct as ever! In a way, I suppose it was. He said you were very young, talked of the future. By implication, asked if my intentions were honourable – and if so, in the context of which of my cultures. But it was not just Leo. Far from it. There were other things at that time. Things were unsettled in my country. I had many personal worries. The future was dark to me. It seemed best to leave before too much harm was done. Let me be direct too. Was too much harm done?'

He leaned forward and looked deep into her eyes.

'Well,' she said shakily. 'It was rather painful at the time. But then, so's toothache.'

He sank back, relieved.

'The so philosophical Zeugma! I have always believed in your resilience.'

She thought, You blind self-satisfied bastard. Don't you know that fat girls have plenty of room to cry inside?

But her pleasure in his company soon soothed her irritation and it was a disappointment when twenty minutes later Amine arrived to announce that dinner was ready.

It was an excellent meal. The main dish was a haunch of spicy venison cooked to a tenderness rare in Zeugma's previous experience of the meat. She ate with relish. Whitethorn had taught her that whatever else a girl might lose there was still hope if she kept her appetite. The others made no effort to keep pace. Hasan ate delicately and led the conversation, quizzing her gently about the site she was working on at the moment. Jonathan was rather withdrawn. He ate mechanically and made do with one small helping. Amine did not even go as far as this, the food on her plate remaining quite untouched. She sat with her elbows on the table, turning a wineglass slowly before her face so that the candlelight by which they ate was caught and broken in the crystal.

She was, Zeugma decided, either a very intelligent woman or one of those hateful creatures possessed of so much natural grace and personality that everything she said sounded knowledgeable and wise. Even with the talk centred on archaeology, Zeugma felt her own expertise was a very small and deep-buried talent.

'This is a *hobby* of yours?' she asked, hoping by the stress to establish something of the gap between the dilettante and the professional.

'An interest only,' said Amine. 'Like Malcolm, I am intrigued. It is Jonathan who is our expert.'

Zeugma looked with surprise at the younger Upas, who was so deep in reverie that even the mention of his name did not rouse him. In repose, his face more than ever seemed familiar.

'I didn't realize,' she said. 'Does he have any special interest?'

Amine pushed a three-stemmed candelabrum towards her brother until the flames flickered so close to his face that their small heat must have been sensible.

His features seemed to rearrange themselves under the moulding touch of the fingers of flame and suddenly he was back with them.

'Forgive me,' he said with a smile of great charm. 'I am being ill-mannered.'

'Yes,' said Amine. 'Your guest was enquiring if your archaeological interests cover any special field.'

'Why yes,' said Upas. 'Did you not know? I am interested mainly in tombs.'

It was an amateurish answer and ought to have given Zeugma some professional reassurance, but instead the word resounded in the air as though it had been spoken in the dry emptiness of a funeral chamber itself.

'Tombs, of course, are a very fruitful source of information and artefacts,' she said in her brightest pedagogic manner. 'But it is the light they throw on the life of a period which makes them so important. Don't you agree?'

'Perhaps,' said Jonathan.

'It is the dangers that attract him, not the scholarship, Miss Gray,' said Amine.

'Dangers?' echoed Zeugma in surprise, looking into the deep dark eyes of the other woman.

'Yes. Like the motor-cycling. To disturb the dead must often be attended by danger. Don't you agree?'

Amine used just enough of Zeugma's own intonation in her question to rouse a suspicion of mockery.

'Oh, you mean the curse of the mummy, all that Hammer Films stuff,' sneered Zeugma in reply.

The remark seemed to fall on fairly stony ground for some reason. They all looked at her in silence and suddenly she had a sense of them as a family, linked by bonds which must forever keep her out. Not that she any longer had any hopes of getting in, she reassured herself.

'Jonathan must show you his museum before you leave us, Miss Gray,' said Amine, breaking the silence.

'You have a museum here?'

'A small collection of little interest to someone familiar with the great museums of the world,' said Jonathan modestly.

'Oh no. Please. I should like to see,' answered Zeugma.

Upas didn't argue and after the meal was over (which meant when Zeugma stopped eating, the others having been mere spectators long before the end) and they had drunk bitter Arab-style coffee in the lounge, he invited her to follow him. Malcolm laughingly refused to join them, saying he had been bored enough in the past by Jonathan's collection of antique crockery. Amine whose supple length elegantly overflowed from an inadequate chaise longue made a gesture which might have been acquiescence or denial and Zeugma who even at White-thorn had always found her appetites to be healthily normal was concerned to realize what an impression Amine's strange beauty was making on her.

The house was quite still, except for the sound of their own steps on the stone-flagged corridor. Somewhere the unobtrusive shadowy-faced woman who had served their food might be closeted with the dishes but the place felt empty.

It was the kind of silence, thought Zeugma, prompted perhaps by her own recent reference to Hammer Films, which seemed created to be broken by a spine-chilling scream.

The mood was maintained by the sight of the huge double door which lay at the end of the passage, its wood darkened beyond identification by age. The lock into which Jonathan now inserted his key was far from an-cient, Zeugma noticed. He must imagine he's got some

144

pretty valuable stuff locked up here, she thought with amusement. But she entered the room with the illogical excitement of an optimistic art dealer climbing to the old attic in which might lie an unrecognized Titian.

Behind her, Jonathan switched on the light and she drew in her breath at what she saw. The room was an unwindowed cube, its only furniture consisting of a tier of four strong wooden shelves which ran round the bare stone walls. These shelves were loaded. When Jonathan said he was interested in tombs, he hadn't been joking. Here were examples of all that vast variety of objects each successive age took with them to the grave like children clutching dolls for comfort in the dark. Weapons and ornaments, crosses and cooking pots, tools and artefacts of all kinds. And among them, more grisly relics still, lay bones. Sternum, clavicle, humerus, scapula, ulna, radius, femur and fibula, the grisly piles lay heaped in every corner, each jauntily surmounted by a skull.

What struck Zeugma at once was the haphazard arrangement of the collection, though a closer inspection made her wonder whether perhaps it was haphazard merely in conventional indexing terms. Certain groupings had an air of the deliberate about them which made her look twice, but the link between, for instance, a medieval dagger and a Middle Bronze Age urn was too idiosyncratic for her comprehension. Something about the urn caught her attention, however, and she was about to remark on it when the door opened and Amine appeared on the threshold. She did not enter but stood in the doorway wrapping her thin arms around her body as though she found the room ineffably cold. Zeugma was surprised by this, as the atmosphere was so comfortably warm that she could not self-deprecatingly put it down to her own superior insulation.

'Yes?' said Upas, sounding annoyed by the interruption.

'Telephone,' she Amine laconically.

Upas did not ask who it was or indeed pass any comment but pushed past his sister with a brusqueness just this side of discourtesy.

Amine remained in the doorway for a moment, then made the smallest of shrugs, a gesture so elegantly expressive that Zeugma felt her mouth corrugate with the lemon-bitterness of envy.

She turned to the urn.

'Has anyone noticed,' she enquired, 'the apparently Roman inscription on the neck of this apparently neolithic urn?'

There was no reply. Amine had gone. Zeugma thrust out her tongue in the direction of the door, a gesture surpassing Amine's in expressiveness at least.

Then she looked at the urn once more, leaning over the table to get a closer view. The inscription was undoubtedly of much later date than the urn. Could the urn have been disinterred twice? Once by some Roman archaeologist, killing time during an overlong posting to the Wall, then a second time two thousand years later by Upas?

She must ask him when he returned. Meanwhile a spot of interpretation might throw some light on the matter.

Carefully she lifted the urn over the other relics and held it up to the light. Something rolled about inside it like a round pebble, but she ignored this, full of disappointment at what a casual glance now told her. The lettering was more recent than two thousand years ago. At a rough guess she'd say it was only a day or two old, hastily and almost illegibly done with a sharp implement. The medieval dagger, perhaps. The inscription was difficut to make out, but Zeugma thought she recognized it as a symbol she recalled seeing fairly often during Pasquino's three-month stay in Italy as a guest of the University of Padua. *Kilroy was here*, Leo had interpreted it. Could Leo have done this? she wondered. She doubted it. He disapproved of those who vandalized history almost as strongly as Zeugma did of those who vandalized the countryside.

Perhaps it was just a whim of Upas'. It was his urn. She made to return it to its place, determined that he should not know of her interest in it. But the rolling sound within made her pause.

Gently she tipped the urn forward. The object inside rolled down the inner curve, hesitated momentarily at the bend of the neck, then plopped heavily on to the shelf. For a moment Zeugma thought it was a child's marble.

Then in the same instant she recognized what it was and whose it was.

It was Leo Pasquino's glass eye.

13

*What Song the Syrens sang, or what
name Achilles assumed when he hid
himself among women, though puzzling
Questions, are not beyond all conjecture.*

The peat fire had broken open and lay like a war-ravaged landscape in the hearth. Peaks and high ground for the moment retained their brown fibrous life but were gradually being subsumed by the red heat below.

Crow sat before the fire, bent forward, peering deep into it like a troubled general poring over a map. He was perfectly still, but Twinkle lying alongside him caught the deep anxieties which beset his master and raised his head, growling.

Crow quietened him with a movement of his hand, then, dissatisfied broke up the fire once more with an old bronze poker. He seemed to like the new disposition even less than the old and rose from his seat and went to the door. The night was dark with cloud, and the rain which had fallen so heavily earlier was now rising again in curls and wraiths of mist. Crow peered into the darkness with the keen-eyed gaze of a watcher on a sunlit peak. North and east he looked as though uncertain which direction commanded his best attention. Once more he returned and stared down into the fire. Once more he went to the door and peered blindly into the darkness.

Twinkle too was on his feet now, scenting an expedition and eager for it. But Crow touched him gently between the eyes and he subsided, showing his disappointment only by a reproachful drooping of his ears.

'I must make up my mind, lad,' said Crow. 'Why do they tell me nowt? Do they think I read thoughts?'

The idea made him smile and the brief moment of humour helped him to come to his decision. He stepped out into the night, chose his direction and started running.

'If I had a hammer,' sang Leo Pasquino.

He really does work at the English eccentric bit, thought Lakenheath disgruntledly. But his real emotional state was still one of mighty relief. It had taken some moments to nerve himself to the point of retrieving his torch and confronting the figure in the cellar once more. This time he quickly took in two reassuring factors previously overlooked. One was that the hands clasped round the boiler pipe were firmly manacled; the second was that what he had taken for some hideous disfigurement of the face was caused partly by a thin piece of cord having been pulled tightly round the mouth and partly by the absence of an eye.

Lakenheath quickly unfastened the gag and if the man's attempts to scrape his manacles open against the pipe were not sufficient evidence of his fortitude, his first words confirmed it.

'That's better. Come along then, quick as you can. The manacles.'

'What?'

'I presume you intend to continue with the work you have so ineptly and belatedly begun?'

'Who are you?' demanded Lakenheath. 'No, don't tell me. The description fits. You must be the absent professor. What's it, Pagliacci.'

'Pasquino. And what kind of anonymous creature are you?'

149

'My name's Lakenheath,' he answered.

This seemed to cause Pasquino some visible amusement.

'Oh, that's who you are? Well, well,' he murmured. 'And how do you know *my* name, or *almost* know it?'

'I'm a friend of Zeugma's,' said Lakenheath, thinking that it was almost true. 'She brought me here tonight.'

'She's not here now?' said Pasquino, alarmed.

'Oh no. She's coming later to pick me up, though.'

'Is she? Good. Then you'd better get to work on those manacles, hadn't you?'

A quick search round the room produced some useful finds – a square-ended spanner which performed some function on the boiler door, a couple of loose bricks and a stub of candle which he lit to save the torch. Next he made Pasquino lie very close to the pipe so that the chain could be spread flat on the stone floor and the spanner used as a chisel with a brick as hammer. The archaeologist favoured a more subtle attack on the lock, but when he realized his arguments were going to be ignored, settled instead for a question-answer session punctuated by bursts of song.

Ten minutes later, visible progress had been made on breaching the metal. But, Lakenheath suddenly realized, while he had been pumped dry of information concerning his presence here, little explanation of Pasquino's much more extraordinary situation had been forthcoming.

He put his feelings into words and Pasquino looked at him with quizzical superiority, rattling his chain as though in hope that it might fall apart. When it didn't, unexpectedly he laughed.

'All right,' he said. 'I daresay ignorance can make you potentially more dangerous than knowledge. But you'll have to keep quiet, you realize that.'

'Scout's honour,' said Lakenheath.

The other man shook his head.

'No. I mean you'll be *made* to keep quiet.'

'What? For God's sake, what are you?'

'Probably the greatest living archaeologist,' said the other modestly. 'Do you think you could go on working while I talk? Thank you. I also do a bit of government work from time to time.'

'Which government? What kind of work?' demanded Lakenheath, wrapping his handkerchief round the brick to protect his blistered hand.

'Oh, your government, mine,' said Pasquino vaguely. 'I travel a lot. It's very expensive. You'd be amazed how much it costs nowadays to maintain even the simplest projects. And the universities and academic grants people are rarely as far-seeing as one would expect. So, as I say, I supplement my resources by doing some government work occasionally.'

'You mean you're some kind of spy?'

'*No*!' He was indignant. 'I have skills. I am perhaps the foremost intuitive reasoner since Newton, I read terrain like a book, I'm an expert at interpreting aerial photographs, I travel widely, I am welcome in ninety per cent of the countries of the world, I meet people. That is all.'

'So who did you come up here to meet? The Upases?'

'So,' said Pasquino. 'You know about them?'

'Zeugma said that was where you were staying.'

'Of course. Well, yes, that was one of the purposes of my visit. I had known them before, or more accurately, known the elder brother, Malcolm. Have you met him?'

'No. Only Jonathan. When Sayer died.'

'Yes. That puzzles me,' said Pasquino. 'Keep hammering, will you? Tell me, has Zeugma had any contact with them?'

'Why yes. She met Jonathan as well. And that's where she is tonight. Having dinner and hoping to meet you.'

'Oh my God!' exclaimed Pasquino, alarmed. 'Why didn't you say? Damnation, can't you get these chains off?'

'What's the trouble?' asked Lakenheath, catching the other's fear. 'There's no danger to Zeugma, is there?'

'Danger?' he answered grimly. 'Where the Upases are, there's always danger. She'll be all right as long as Malcolm's there. He's a cool head, a businessman. But those other two, they're something else. Listen, I'd better fill you in completely so you're under no illusions. Anyway, I suppose you've got a right to know.'

'What do you mean by that?' asked Lakenheath, alarmed.

Pasquino looked at him with a disturbing kind of sympathy.

'I'll start at the beginning. Keep hammering, will you? Speed is of the essence. I first met Upas, Malcolm that is, over ten years ago, in Damascus. He was a friend of one of my friends, an interesting young man, well educated, rich, charming. He seemed to have got the best out of both his heritages. I didn't see him again until several years later when I was back in the Middle East in Cairo. Zeugma was with me then. Upas appeared, or Hasan as he was calling himself then. The British part of his heritage had become somewhat devalued in Arab eyes in the intervening years and he asked me to stick to his Arab name, which I did. Well, pretty soon he began to get very close to Zeugma and I felt it my duty to keep some kind of eye on the situation.'

'You mean they had an affair?' asked Lakenheath. 'And you interfered?'

'I am her guardian,' said Pasquino, indignantly. 'In any case, all my interference consisted of was bringing Upas's name into a conversation I had with a contact of mine in the Egyptian government. His reaction was sufficient to make me institute further enquiries through other channels.'

'Other channels?'

'Oh, friends, diplomats, local gossips,' said Pasquino vaguely. 'What I learned made me determined to break up this relationship straightaway. Upas, Malcolm that is, moved in all the best circles in most Middle Eastern capitals. He entertained lavishly, catering for all his guests' needs. *All.* You understand? To cut a long story short, my information was that Upas made his money out of running an agency for blackmail material. Note the way I put it. He was never connected directly with any black-mail attempt. But a young diplomat or foreign business-man might wake up on the morning after a Upas party feeling rather worried about the previous night's excesses. But as days, weeks, months, years even, pass they fade to just a pleasant memory. Until one day he becomes im-portant, or is posted somewhere important, or his firm makes an important discovery. He might even feel his new responsibilities strongly, resolve to lead a discreet, blame-less life henceforth. But it's too late. The evidence exists, film, tape, a full dossier. And it comes into the hands of the highest bidder.'

'But that's monstrous!' exclaimed Lakenheath. 'And pretty far-fetched. What about the two younger Upases? They must have been just kids five, six years ago.'

'Precocious kids,' said Pasquino grimly. 'Malcolm liked to keep it in the family. Cut down on overheads, I sup-pose. It was nothing but a business to him, but those two developed a taste for the exotic at an early stage. I've seen some of the pictures.'

Lakenheath launched a violent attack on the visibly weakening chain, putting Pasquino's wrists at consider-able risk.

'Hold it! Hold it!' he protested. 'I said hurry, but I may have need of my hands on some future occasion.'

'We've got to get Zeugma out of there,' said Laken-heath.

'You like her, do you?'

'Well, yes. I suppose I do, in a way,' answered Laken-heath, pausing. 'Brotherly, you understand.'

'I understand. Listen, don't be over-anxious. This man

Malcolm, he liked her too, I really believe that. I got some friends to apply a bit of pressure so that he had to leave Cairo in a hurry. It really shook Zeugma up, but I got her out of there pretty quickly too, intercepted a couple of letters he tried to get to her and the thing eventually died. But what I'm trying to say is, he's got no reason to harm her and quite a lot of reason to keep her healthy. So don't worry.'

'Okay,' said Lakenheath. 'And what about you? What reason has he got for harming you?'

'That's easy. The Upases used their father's family house as a kind of holiday home, a bolt-hole if you like. We know there have been pressures put on Malcolm to let it be used in all kinds of ways. It'd make a useful centre for guerrilla groups, a bomb-factory, any fanatic revolutionary activity that Arabs – and others – might get up to. But he's resisted, successfully to date. But he couldn't stop Amine and Jonathan getting up to their old tricks. They're rather afraid of him, though, and to make their activities seem relatively business-like, they involved one of the scientists working here at Thirlsike.'

'Healot,' interrupted Lakenheath.

'Right. You're beginning to see a pattern,' said the other approvingly. 'Malcolm was furious when he found out, but decided to make the best of a bad job. Then a girl was killed.'

Lakenheath stopped hammering and became very still.

'A local girl. Sharon Anderson. God knows what happened, but Healot was certainly mixed up in it with Jonathan and his sister. Healot got out quickly. The centre was being run down at that time, so it didn't look too odd. He made for the States, again a natural thing to do if you've been treated the way that most of the best minds get treated in this country. I should know. Well, Healot dropped right into a comfortable, well-paid and highly elevated post in the middle of some nasty American desert. They had been after him for some time, it seems.

But the local ladies' social committee welcome party wasn't all that was waiting for him out there. A lot of Healot material had already been bought from the Upases on spec and the poor blighter quickly discovered he had taken on two jobs, one with the American government, and the other with a rather different body of men. Or perhaps not so very different after all.'

'You mean he was blackmailed to pass information as soon as he got there?' said Lakenheath. 'Christ, no wonder the poor bastard hanged himself!'

Pasquino laughed.

'Oh no. You've got it wrong. Healot was no guilt-ridden neurotic. He was a very able, very self-controlled man, except for one unfortunate appetite, of course. He knew enough about security techniques to be suspicious when helpful acquaintances started offering him his own particular forbidden fruits by the treeful. So he probably gave the Upas residence a good going over when he was there one night. His suspicions would have been confirmed. Cameras, tape-recorders, two-way mirrors – I've no doubt he found all the equipment.'

'Then why the hell did he carry on?' demanded Lakenheath, hammering with growing urgency.

'Presumably,' said Pasquino, 'because he found something else which made him feel powerful enough to resist any pressures the Upases might bring to bear.'

'What would that be?'

'I suspect it was some form of record they kept of all their material. As I said before, some of it wouldn't be used for years – then suddenly its market price would rocket as Mr X became Minister of Defence. Now, we know Healot himself was a dab hand with a camera. My theory is that he photographed this material and put it away for a rainy day. Well, the rain came as soon as he reached the States. So he probably phoned or cabled the Upases suggesting that if the pressure continued on him, he would knock the bottom out of their business by releasing copies of their records to all interested parties. No one buys what everyone's got. What he didn't take into account was that the Upases had no control over material once it was sold and that their customers felt little sense of moral obligation to anyone. In other words, there was no way of stopping the blackmailers.'

'Except,' said Lakenheath slowly, 'by removing the object of the blackmail.'

'Bright boy. One of them – Jonathan, I suspect, as it was a botched-up job – arranged to meet Healot. What happened at that meeting is hard to say. We can only guess. But at the end of it Healot was dangling from a skylight in a hotel bathroom.'

'And Upas had the photos?'

'No. We think not. In fact we're certain. Don't ask me how. They'd be too dangerous for Healot to carry around with him, especially going to America. Their Customs officers are ferocious seekers after the odd. So he left them here.'

'In England.'

'Warm,' said Pasquino. 'In this centre, I believe, or close by. He had an odd sense of humour, Healot. You know, when this place was built, they unearthed an urn-field. Most of the stuff went to the museum at Carlisle. But one not very important urn was kept here, as a kind of memorial, I suppose. Well, that urn disappeared just before Healot left. One of his former colleagues recalls mentioning it to Healot at his farewell party and getting the reply, "There're some ashes stay warmer than others and it's not just Pharaoh's tomb that's got its curse." An odd comment.'

'Hardly odd enough to be committed to memory,' observed Lakenheath.

'Efficient questioning leaves no stone unturned,' said Pasquino. 'Anyway, it seemed worthwhile having a look around up here. It would fit what we know of Healot's interests for him to have dropped the photos into this urn and re-buried it somewhere safe. They didn't want a full-scale search. No, it was a job for a single expert. So naturally they called on me. I was rather short of funds and I have in mind some rather expensive submarine excavations. Camelot, I believe, will be found beneath the Solway Firth. Those people at Cadbury are wasting their time. So I accepted the task. I should know better at my age.'

'But where did you start? Here at the centre? I mean, what were you looking for?'

Pasquino sighed, as if he did not particularly wish to carry on along this particular avenue.

'I had some pictures, aerial photos, for a start . . .'

'Mine!' exclaimed Lakenheath, recalling Zeugma's reaction when she saw the photos in his office. 'I bet they were mine.'

'Yes. Well, I believe they did contrive some other reason for having them taken.'

'Contrive!'

But Pasquino was pressing on now at full speed.

'I examined them carefully. You can tell a great deal from such pictures, you know. Particularly when you have a full range in different lights. I spotted all kinds of interesting archaeological features, and got Zeugma started on a dig at some of these promising sites. Then I strolled off to take a look at another area which looked disturbed to me. But much more recently disturbed. I wasn't particularly hopeful. It could have been anything. Almost immediately I started digging, I thought I was on to something. There was an urn there, or rather a bell beaker, but it was nothing like the urn I had expected to find. But curiously it contained something modern; flour. Recently ground. I realized I was at a burial site. A curious mish-mash of forms, but early Bronze Age mainly. Only the bodies were far from Bronze Age. I only saw a girl but there were others.'

'A girl?' said Lakenheath. But he did not really need

to say anything. He understood now Pasquino's reluctance to continue.

'Yes. I fear that she may have been your cousin,' said Pasquino, forthright now he had reached this point.

'Yes,' said Lakenheath. 'Yes.'

He sat quite still for a while and the other man offered no complaint at this cessation of work.

'How did she die?' he asked finally.

'I don't know. I was interrupted. Jonathan Upas came across me. I guessed who he was, and he seemed to know me. When he saw what I had discovered, he couldn't let me go, of course. He made me cover up the small section of earth I had disturbed. Then he performed some strange antics over it, muttering away like one of Macbeth's witches. He's the worst kind of sadist, I feel. He believes there's more to his violence than his own personal pleasure.'

'Crow said he felt close for a while, then it went away again,' murmured Lakenheath. 'He must be a force to be reckoned with, this Upas.'

He nodded as though affirming a promise.

'Crow?' said Pasquino. 'So you've met that old charlatan. A great fund of knowledge there, great. But he's got no time scale, none at all. I honestly doubt if he knows what century he's in!'

'What happened next?' asked Lakenheath, resuming his assault on the chains.

'I was taken to their house where I met Malcolm again. It was quite clear they too had heard about Healot's urn and had stayed on in Liddesdale in an effort to locate it. Their researches had been concentrated mainly within the centre itself.'

'Yes. I saw Healot's room.'

'A vain effort, but not entirely misplaced, I suspect. Doubtless this was when they encountered your cousin and her friends. Perhaps their first meeting was friendly enough. But once the Upases discovered how relatively disconnected they were and also that Sayer had warned them off, then they became the perfect victims. A necessity in Malcolm's eyes, a pleasure for those other two. So everyone was pleased and no questions asked.'

'But I was asking questions,' said Lakenheath.

'Yes, I suppose you were,' said Pasquino thoughtfully. 'Tell me, you look as if you might have had an accident recently.'

'Yes. I did as a matter of fact. Very minor . . .'

'And this man, Sayer. He was driving the car you normally drive when he crashed?'

'Oh Christ,' said Lakenheath. 'Then Zeugma was right. And Jonathan . . . ?'

'Yes. Far from trying to pull Sayer out, he was probably making bloody sure he stayed in!'

The anger in Lakenheath was now burning bright through all his body. He brought the brick down hard, once, twice, and the chain parted.

'Well, thank you for that,' said Pasquino, stretching his arms and luxuriating in his new-found freedom. 'You wouldn't happen to have a Burmese cheroot on your person, would you? Or a flask of brandy?'

'I've got some Scotch upstairs,' said Lakenheath.

'Well, that will do, I daresay. And then we must organize ourselves.'

'Yes. But you still haven't said why you're here.'

'Haven't I? Oh no. Well the thing is, I was foolish enough to let myself be provoked into hinting at my own theory which is that the urn must be *in* the centre. I did it as a double-bluff, to make them concentrate their attention on the outer terrain. But Malcolm's very astute. He brought me here, tried a little elementary torture, but it's not really his line. Then tied me up as you saw and said he'd be back later. No doubt he intends to bring something of Zeugma's and threaten me with some harm to her.'

'But you said . . .'

'Oh, never fear. It'll be a bluff, I think.'

'But you'd tell him what you think you know?'

'Would I, young man?' asked Pasquino. 'I'm not sure. Once I talk, I'm dead, you realize that. It's only my gratitude to you that makes me tolerate your stupid questions. Though I might still have wriggled out somehow. I'm fairly ingenious.'

He laughed.

'They locked me in young Upas's so-called museum. What chaos! I took my glass eye out and dropped it into a rather nice mid-bronze urn and scratched a little latin sign on the neck. Who knows? Some bright policeman might notice it. It's remarkable what little clues an alert mind can leave to its passage.'

He preened himself and rose, staggering slightly and grabbing hold of the boiler for support. He was still very weak.

'What if Zeugma spots your sign and finds your eye?' asked Lakenheath.

'What? If that happened and they knew it had happened, then she would be in the very greatest danger,' said Pasquino.

'Let's go,' said Lakenheath, beset suddenly by strong premonitions of disaster.

'Wait!' hissed Pasquino. 'Did you hear something?'

'No. Where?'

'Through the door. On the stair.'

They listened together. The silence was so complete that after a while it became more menacing than any noise could be.

'You were mistaken,' said Lakenheath firmly. But he took up the candle and moved with great caution to the doorway, peering up the length of stairs to the paler darkness of the open door at their head. His view was uninterrupted.

'There. Nothing,' he said, turning back to Pasquino. But as he turned he sensed a movement behind the door, span round to see a figure emerging and leapt forward to grapple with it. The candle flame wavered wildly in the draught from the movement illuminating the face before him like a cloud-swept landscape.

It was Diss.

In his hands he held the shotgun whose acquaintance Lakenheath had already made. The barrel came up and he had time to feel that this might be his last moment in this most beautiful and deadly of worlds. Then Diss brought the barrel round in a short arc which ended at the side of Lakenheath's head and he sank to the ground in a darkness more complete than that caused by the failing of his candle.

And out on the moor Crow was running beneath a wild sky, muscles and lungs strained to bursting-point, and in his ice-cold mind the growing conviction that he had delayed too long.

14

The dead seem all alive in the human
Hades of Homer, yet cannot well speak,
prophesie, or know the living, except
they drink blood . . .

Nothing she had learned at Whitethorn nor anything she
had experienced since had equipped Zeugma to deal with
a situation like this.

Her first reaction was that it was some grotesque joke,
but this theory did not begin to make sense. Such sense
of humour as Leo possessed travelled in directions quite
opposite to this. Perhaps, though, it wasn't his joke. Upas's
then? But you didn't separate a man from his glass eye
without his co-operation. (Unless he were dead, said a
traitor's voice in her mind, but she ignored it.)

No, Leo must have put it there himself, and scratched
the inscription on the urn too.

But to what end? To tell anyone clever enough and
lucky enough to spot the urn and find its contents that
Leo Pasquino had been here? But she knew he had been
here. It was no secret. So why . . . ?

She looked round the room as if it might give her an
answer. And suddenly it did. Not an answer she liked, but
one which fitted. This big, solid, windowless room with
its formidable door was no longer an amateur archaeologist's museum. It was a cell, a prison. Put anyone in

here and there was no hope of getting out. And what did the prisoners do? They scratched messages, tried to leave some trace of themselves; especially when their case was hopeless . . . No! this *is* absurd, she told herself. And looking at the door as she did so, she felt herself grow weak with fear at the conviction that it was now locked. So strong was this feeling that it hardly seemed worth taking the half-dozen paces necessary to check the truth. Somehow she forced her legs to carry her to the door, seized the metal ring which served instead of a knob, and pulled.

The door swung easily open without a sound, and she heard herself sob reflexively with relief.

So it had all been nonsense. But the small sphere of glass in her hand was real enough. That needed an explanation. She strode determinedly down the corridor in search of it.

Her life seemed to be a series of confrontations. The fairy who dished out diplomacy must have been unable to get near her cradle. Though God knows why, she thought bitterly. There could hardly have been a crush of generous donors!

She had long ago analysed that her lack of subtlety rose from fear. Anything less than confrontation smacked of evasion, and on the battlefield which she felt her life to be, even reasonable compromise loomed like defeat.

So now, with heart beating faster, a nervous sweat prickling under her arms, a deeper flush suffusing her rosy cheeks, she strode up to the lounge door. It was ajar. She thrust it open without breaking her stride and prepared to do battle.

So wrought up to combat readiness was she that it took a good ten seconds for two fairly obvious factors to make themselves felt.

First of all, the room was empty.

Secondly, it was not the lounge.

This room, lit only by a pleasant smelling wood-fire,

seemed at first glance to be a study. The panelled walls on either side of the fireplace were lined with books and the other walls were hung with pictures whose subject matter the shifting shadows did not permit her to discern. But there were no desks or chairs. Indeed there was no furniture of any kind and the stone-flagged floor was devoid of any form of carpeting.

The lounge in which she had drunk her coffee must, she surmised, be the next room along the corridor. In fact, she now recalled a door at the end of the lounge which presumably led into this room and as her eyes grew accustomed to the dim light, she tried to spot the door in what at first glance looked like uninterrupted panelling. So well camouflaged was it that she had to approach the wall to convince herself that there was really a door there. The door knob was counter-sunk so that no protrusion spoilt the line of the panel, and her fingers, lightly caressing the grain of the wood, touched and shifted a small panel which swivelled over the key-hole. Through the hole thus revealed came a ray of light and on an impulse she dropped on one knee and peered through.

She had been right. It was the lounge she found herself looking into, and the three Upases were there. Or at least two of them certainly were. Amine's head she could see resting against the end of the chaise longue. Jonathan seemed to be sitting on the floor beside her and they were both looking attentively towards their left, clearly listening to somebody, presumably Malcolm. To confirm this, Zeugma switched from eye to ear. At first all she got was a shell-like effect of the roar of the sea, but then by chance she found the optimum acoustic angle and voices came through fairly loud and clear.

Malcolm was speaking. The voice still sent a frisson of something over her body. Was it desire? Could she possibly still love him? But now the sense of his words began to cause other feelings.

'I think she knows nothing,' said Malcolm. 'But even if

she isn't completely ignorant, it's still better to leave her alone.'

'This sounds almost sentimental, my brother.'

Jonathan's voice, mocking.

'No. I do what I do on rational grounds, not for my own indulgence.'

Malcolm again, contemptuous.

'In this case, you may be right. She can offer little to a man of your well-known aesthetic sensitivity.'

A pause. Zeugma risked missing something and took a quick look through the key-hole. Malcolm had now moved into the picture and was stooping down over Jonathan. His voice when she heard it again was so cold and menacing as to be almost unrecognizable.

'. . . troubles come from your self-indulgence. You are as foolish and as dangerous as the seller of opium who is also an addict. Believe me, you shall not destroy me with you. Amine, my sister, control him !'

'We all do what we must. You too, my brother.'

Amine spoke in Arabic, but her words were easy enough for Zeugma to translate. The first part was a version of a common proverb. The term she used which Zeugma rendered to herself as 'my brother' was the respectful form of address used towards the head of a household. Its intention she suspected was ironic.

'I must go now. You will make my apologies to the girl. And you will send her home. Tomorrow or the day after, she will hear the sad news.'

'The car again?'

Amine.

'Yes. But this time, efficiently.'

'It was *my* arms which got burnt !'

Jonathan, querulously.

Malcolm uttered an expletive which it would have taken a lexicon of four-letter words to translate and the lounge door slammed.

'He grows tedious !'

165

The outburst was Jonathan's.

'He is like our father. A man of prudence and reason. And he is right, Jonathan. Without him, we would find it hard. Do not cross him in this matter of the girl.'

'But the time is right.'

'Times return. We will find other times.'

Silence again.

Zeugma pressed her eye to the key-hole once more. Jonathan was kneeling before Amine, who held his head in between her hands and looked deep into his eyes. Slowly she drew him towards her and they met in an embrace that was far from brotherly.

Shocked by this, and sorely puzzled by what she had heard, Zeugma pushed herself upright to discover she had got pins-and-needles in the leg she had been kneeling on. It buckled under her and she staggered against the door. At the same time, the glass eye slipped from her hand and bounced like a marble across the stone floor.

The reaction of the Upases must have been instantaneous. The eye was still bouncing when the door from the lounge was flung open. Jonathan stood there and Zeugma smiled weakly at him, her mind desperately seeking a plausible story and her eye measuring the distance to the doorway into the corridor. But explanation and escape were cut off by Amine's appearance there. She entered the room stooped gracefully, and picked up the glass eye.

'Please may I have that,' said Zeugma, after a long moment's silence. 'It's Leo's spare eye. I brought it with me in case he needed it.'

All things considered, she felt it wasn't a bad try, but it did not win the applause it merited.

Amine held the eye up for Jonathan to see. A strange and disquieting half-smile played round her lips.

'Brother,' she said. 'I think the case has altered.'

'And she was listening,' responded Jonathan. 'Nor is

she as stupid as she looks. She must understand something of this.'

'To understand even a little is dangerous.'

'So we cannot let her go.'

'No, we cannot let her go.'

Zeugma wished she could find this casual assumption of power over her amusing, but instead she found it chilled her genial spirits and filled her with foreboding. This exchange between brother and sister sounded both tentative and purposeful as though they were casting around for a logical sequential path to carry them over uncertain ground to a longed-for destination. Somehow Zeugma did not fancy getting there. In this case she felt sure it was better to travel despairingly than to arrive.

'What of Malcolm?' asked Jonathan next. It was the first hopeful thing Zeugma had heard.

Amine shook her head impatiently. Their roles, Zeugma noticed, seemed to have been reversed, Jonathan was now the hesitant one, concerned about his elder brother's reaction, while Amine who had previously counselled caution, was all for pressing on – with what?

'He will be late,' she said dismissively. 'First to the town, then to the centre. It may be morning before he returns.'

The centre. What the hell did Malcolm want at the centre? wondered Zeugma. And what *would* he do when he found Lakenheath there?

But Lakenheath would have to fend for himself. This cold debate, which concerned her so closely and which she found herself powerless to join was coming to a climax.

'Must we wait?'

'The season is ripe,' said Amine.

'The day is ripe,' agreed Jonathan.

And Zeugma found herself recalling that it was the first day of spring.

'I don't know what you're talking about,' she said

stiffly. 'But it really is rather late and I think I'd better be going now.'

They continued to ignore her, both turning and locking their respective doors. Zeugma went from one to the other, trying them, still at the stage where her fear of making herself ridiculous was sufficient to restrain her mounting hysteria.

'Please open these doors,' she said in her best White-thorn She-who-must-be-obeyed voice, reserved for complaints about bad service in restaurants and shops.

The two still ignored her, but they **did** open a door, a hitherto unsuspected one in the wall opposite the lounge door, and passed through into a small chamber. Zeugma did not attempt to follow immediately but did a quick tour of the room to see if it held any other concealed exits. If there were any, she could not find them, and what she did find was little to her comfort. The books were a comprehensive library of the occult, ranging from scholarly works like Professor Thorndike's eight volume *History of Magic* and *Experimental Science* through the allegedly practical and autobiographic works of modern magicians like Levi and Crowley to what were clearly very valuable copies, often handwritten, of *grimoires*, or magical textbooks. Graeco-Egyptian texts abounded, some in specially designed perspex containers and of such obvious antiquity that Zeugma began to wonder just how far Jonathan's tomb-collecting activities extended. Set into the wall above the fireplace was a relief carving in sandstone of a bull being killed by a young man whose features were disturbingly like Jonathan's. It seemed likely that it had come from a Mithraic temple and Zeugma felt the serious archaeologist's pang of indignation at the thought that this and other finds may have been stolen for personal delectation rather than exhumed in the interests of science.

But there was little room amid her growing anxieties for such unselfish emotions. She now saw that what she had thought were pictures on the walls were for the most part charts and diagrams, incomprehensible geometric shapes, symbols, patterns of letters, lists of names. But there was one picture, or piece of tapestry rather, in a deep red silk thread on a dark background, the pattern almost invisible at first, but as she looked, the light seemed to pick out and be reflected from the glossier silk and a picture emerged. It was a winged goat with a human body. On its forehead between the great curving horns was a pentagram or five-pointed star. The body had the breasts of a woman and a formalised male organ, erect and entwined by two snakes. The thighs and lower legs were goat-like again, ending in cloven hooves. It was a powerful albeit revolting piece of work and Zeugma found she had spent longer than she intended standing before it.

She shook her head angrily. No wonder Malcolm felt the need to exercise such control over his younger brother and sister, if these were the kind of childish, self-indulgent pastimes they pursued. And she was angry at herself for her own passivity. It was time to leave. If they tried to stop her, they'd have a fight on their hands. And at White-thorn while they taught you that ladies *didn't* fight, they also taught you the concomitant lesson, that if you did have to fight, you needn't do it like a lady.

She pushed open the door of the side chamber, and stopped dead.

It was lit by candles, huge church candles she suspected. But it wasn't these that held her attention. Amine and Jonathan were there. And they were both naked.

Amine knelt before her brother, not in a posture of adoration but because she seemed to be giving him a sponge-down from a basin of water she carried, and apparently she had reached his legs. The rest of his body gleamed damply, as did hers.

Zeugma prided herself on being a tolerant liberal being, but this she found too much. Besides, indignation was a good emetic for fear.

'For God's sake!' she said in disgust. 'You must please yourselves, of course. But I'm leaving!'

They paid her no attention still; Amine continued her careful washing, Jonathan seemed to be in a semi-trance. The bare stonewalled chamber they were in offered even less in the way of possible exits than the other room and Zeugma turned and ran back in to see if she could force a way out. Neither of the two locked doors reacted in the slightest to her solid shoulder charges and all the physical effort did was to cause her enough pain to let fear come rushing back in.

She began to hunt around for something she could use as a weapon for an assault on the woodwork of the doors or, even though she still tried to refuse to admit this possibility, to protect herself. There was nothing. No fire-irons, no furniture, nothing.

Amine entered, still naked, and with a grace of movement and posture few women achieve even expertly clothed and rehearsed, she placed the two huge candles on either side of the goat-tapestry. She went into the small chamber again, returning almost instantly with a bowl the contents of which she proceeded to sprinkle on the fire. It crackled and spat and burnt with a blue flame, emitting a pungent sulphurous smell admixed with traces of camphor and, more faintly still, laurel.

Zeugma had had enough.

'Look here, Amine,' she said, grasping at the woman's arm as she passed. But the washing ceremony must have involved an oiling of the body too, for her grip slipped vainly on the smooth skin and at the same time a wisp of the fumes from the fire caught at her throat and doubled her up in a fit of choking and coughing.

When she recovered, Jonathan was in the room. Her basic prudery made her glad to observe that he at least was now clothed, though his chosen dress was not reassuring. It was a single black khaftan-like garment which fell almost to the floor. In a way, it was remarkably becoming and he wore it with the ease of one used to robes. Most Europeans out of trousers and jacket look as if their backbones have been liquified, but Jonathan looked as if he could stride across the desert with the best. Unfortunately sun and sand were a million miles away and in this darksome room the robe spoke of other more fearful traditions.

Jonathan had stooped to the floor on which he was drawing something with a large block of chalk. He was in fact, Zeugma realized, following an outline already traced on the floor or perhaps imperfectly erased after a previous ceremony.

So, they played these black-magic games, thought Zeugma. What role they proposed for her was not yet clear, but she doubted whether it was intended to be a very comfortable one. So far, neither of them had attempted any physical intimidation which, she assured herself grimly, was just as well for them. And if they thought they were going to put the frights on her by thought alone, they had better think again.

Jonathan had completed a circle with his chalk, all except a small arc of about eighteen inches. He was now carefully drawing another shape inside and contingent with the circle. It consisted of two interlocking triangles, forming a six-pointed star.

'Ah,' said Zeugma brightly. 'I see you prefer the hexagram to the pentagram. The Seal of Solomon, isn't it?'

Amine now reappeared carrying with her a small brazier which she set in the hexagon formed by the intersection of the triangles. She was careful to enter the circle through the gap left by her brother which he now carefully filled in, and though only a thin line of chalk separated her from them, Zeugma felt a chilling sense of exclusion.

Jonathan now moved slowly around the circle, anticlockwise, pausing four times raising his clasped hands above his head and gabbling some incantation with the speed and inaudibility of a parson eager to get morning service over and head for the golf course. The likeness amused Zeugma and she made herself laugh out loud to demonstrate her amusement. The sound jarred; either the room's acoustics of her vocal cords were not fitted for laughter.

Amine meanwhile knelt by the brazier and blew gently on the contents which from the even redness of the respondent glow seemed to be charcoal. She really was incredibly attractive, thought Zeugma. Every line of her body was smooth and taut without any bit of athletic muscularity. School captains like this would have been easy to love.

Now the brazier glowed bright and the woman rose and started sifting on to it handfuls of material she drew from a small black satchel. Clouds of dark grey smoke began to rise and rapidly spread, filling the room with pungent, acrid fumes which made those previously emanating from the fire seem like attar of roses.

Through the swirling smoke and its resultant tears, it was almost impossible to see the figures in the circle, but Zeugma heard Jonathan's voice, no longer gabbling but resounding loud and clear.

'I conjure thee, O Euronymous, Prince of Death, I conjure thee, strengthened by the power of Almighty God, and I command thee by Baralmensis, Baldachiensis, Paumachie, Apolorosedes, and the most powerful Princes Genio and Liachide, Ministers of the Seat of Tartarus and . . . '

Now a new bout of coughing prevented Zeugma from hearing any more and she moved away to the furthermost corner of the room in an effort to avoid the fumes. It wasn't just the discomfort she feared; her knowledge of so-called magical rites was sketchy, but she knew that the numerous eye-witness accounts of successful spirit-raising had to be explained as hallucinations rather than frauds. Self-induced hysteria alone could result in visual delusions, but it seemed likely that some external help was given and the brazier was the most probable source. She was not expert enough to identify whatever it was Amine was sprinkling into the red glow of the charcoal; it might contain Indian hemp, hemlock, black hellebore, henbane (what an evil letter H was, she thought reproachfully) or any combination of narcotic plants known and unknown.

A clever idea suggested itself to her and she made for the small inner chamber, hoping to find refuge if not an escape route. It was difficult to see, or indeed to recollect, where the door was, but by pressing herself against the wall (whose smooth panelling seemed to yield and mould itself most sensuously against her body) she was able to edge her way round the room till she found it.

It was locked. Of course. She felt no surprise. Her mind, still in control, had expected this. Now it must work at other ideas. She sat down on the floor – to get beneath the fumes, she told herself – but the cloying smoke wreaths were heavier than air; had she forgotten those smelly laboratory classes where in a few dull hours Whitethorn girls learned everything about science a lady needed to know? She tried to rise again, but the effort was hard and her body seemed ponderous and bulky beyond even the worst fears of her teenage nightmares.

Jonathan's voice still continued; it had risen in pitch and anger. Euronymous, Prince of Death, seemed reluctant to put in an appearance (perhaps the poor sod's got stuck in the Underground rush-hour, giggled Zeugma to herself) and Upas was threatening all kinds of unpleasantness, backing up these threats with 'the Most High Names of God, *Hain, Lon, Hilay, Sabaoth, Helim, Radisha . . .*' *Radisha* started her giggling again and she missed a couple *. . . Tetragrammaton, Sadai . . .*' It really was too like a Czechoslovakian football team; *now a long ball from Hilay finds Agios, he crosses to Helim who beats two, three defenders, chips on to the head of Tetragrammaton and it's there! England are out of the Underworld Cup by a narrow fifteen-goal margin!*

But jokes are nothing if not shared, and Zeugma began to crawl forward to let the Upases know how ridiculous they were. The smoke cleared a little and she saw them now, he with his arms stretched wide and the skin of his face taut and death-pale, she alongside him, her body a-shine with oil and perspiration, and rounded and soft-looking now, as though ready for the act of love.

What's it all about? Zeugma asked herself. Why all this jiggery-pokery and gobble-de-gook? No one's shown any desire to tie me to a cross and rape me. Or to cut me in half with a magic sword. Why?

'Am I not good enough?' she shouted indignantly, but it came out as an incoherent screech.

Her cry seemed to urge them on to redouble their efforts. Jonathan's voice rose to a scream Amine's body was shaken by some vast internal convulsion as she poured more and more of her odoriferous fuel on the charcoal fire.

It's too simple, thought Zeugma. They're trying to frighten me! They get their kicks from seeing me terrified. Them in their circle, me out here with the demons. Euronymous gets to grips with me, and they . . . well, it might come to incest, but at the moment they both look as if they can manage very well by themselves. When old Euronymous shows up, they'll probably explode!

She threw her head back and laughed, but again the sound was not quite right. The tone of Jonathan's voice had changed. Still commanding, it no longer threatened, but began to sound approving, almost welcoming. Uneasily Zeugma glanced over her shoulder. Nothing was there. Just smoke. Then the wall. And on the wall the goat tapestry between the two candles.

Her gaze focussed on this; the pattern was almost invisible and she felt some compulsion to try to pick it out. And as she watched, it was as if an electric current passed slowly along a filament, for the silken thread of the picture began to glow, softly at first but with ever-increasing radiance, brighter and brighter, till it seemed as if the monstrous outline was detached from it background and floated in air, a hideous luminescent apparition.

An illusion, Zeugma told herself, a simple illusion. But suddenly it seemed best of all ideas to get into the circle with the Upases, who were at least, if perhaps a trifle over-obviously, flesh and blood.

She turned once more and resumed her crawl. She could see them clearly, their eyes fixed on her slow-moving body, their faces alight with evil joy and triumph.

Damn them! she thought. They shan't see me afraid.

She halted. Glanced over her shoulder. The shape of the goat was gaining bulk and substance. The red eyes glowed and moved and fixed themselves on her own. The snakes encircling the penis raised their heads, darted long forked tongues and hissed.

It was no time for pride. She couldn't take her eyes off the goat, but now she pushed herself backwards towards the circle, bringing her knees up to her chest, then straightening her legs, like an oarsman on his slide. Her long skirt was a hindrance, so she dragged it up over her thighs and thought she detected a visible reaction in the goat. I suppose I should feel gratified, she told herself in a desperate effort at cheerfulness. Especially when the competition is Amine, starkers.

But Amine was in the circle, out of reach. This goat was clearly a pragmatist. She pushed back desperately once more. Surely she must be there now? And her back struck something so solid she felt sure she must have missed her direction and come up against the wall.

But a glance over her shoulder showed her she had not been wrong. She was at the circle's edge. The two Upases towered over her, huge beyond mere human dimension, gleeful beyond human joy, but still preferable still infinitely preferable to the obscene horror which filled the room behind her. She thrust herself against the circle once

175

more. There was nothing there, no visible barrier, yet she could not cross the chalk line.

She heard herself making screaming noises again. There was some small satisfaction in this. At least she wasn't trying to laugh or to speak – this time she was just trying to scream.

The goat-monster was almost on her now. She tried to close her eyes to it, but couldn't. Perhaps the Turkish Officers' Manual was a work of compassion after all; perhaps blindness in these circumstances was a blessing; perhaps . . .

No! This was submission! Whitethorn girls did not submit. If devils could seek the pleasures of the flesh, presumably they could also feel the pains of the flesh. And in all conscience the target was huge enough.

Supporting herself against the invisible barrier round the circle, she kicked upwards with all her strength between the monstrous, hairy and scaled goat-legs.

At the same moment, with a noise like an explosion, the corridor door burst open and a blast of cold, fresh air swept across the room, dispersing the brazier fumes and blowing out the candles. Zeugma's foot met nothing, the barrier behind her dissolved and she fell backwards into the circle, from which undignified recumbent position she saw that the goat was once more just an almost invisible tapestry pattern, the Upases had resumed normal human dimensions, and standing in the open door, his face strained and white as though from some great effort of will and strength was Crow.

15

*The number of the dead long exceedeth
all that shall live. The night of time far
surpasseth the day and who knows when
was the Aequinox?*

Zeugma's first reaction was to shout with joy. They had
been right after all at Whitethorn. Virtue *would* triumph;
the U.S. Calvary *did* arrive in the nick of time.

But, she quickly realized, in the present case there was
something not quite right. Whereas the mere sound of
bugles was generally enough to send the Indians running,
the Upases did not look terrified but full of rage.

Crow advanced into the room, his steps slow and difficult, almost as if he had been drinking. Zeugma would
not have blamed him if he'd felt it necessary to down a
gallon or so of his brose before coming to the rescue. But
clearly he was in no state to effect the rescue unaided.

This was underlined by Jonathan, who leapt out of
the circle and with contemptuous ease caught Crow's
outstretched arm in a judo lock and flung him against
the wall. With difficulty Zeugma pushed herself up from
the ground and staggered to Crow's aid, but a hand seized
her by her short unruly hair and forced her head backwards till she was staring, pop-eyed, up into Amine's face.

Zeugma looked at her more in sorrow than anger. She
really was beautiful. But the one thing that Zeugma had
been best at at Whitethorn was fighting and she had never

found the beauty of her opponents anything but an advantage. Carefully she reached up with her hands clasped them behind Amine's neck and brought the exquisitely sculpted head swinging down so that the long, delicate nose crashed solidly into her forehead.

Amine screamed, released her grip on Zeugma's hair, put her hands to her face for an instant, then stared unbelievingly at the sticky redness which stained them.

During this instant Zeugma turned, picked a spot midway between the navel and the mound of Venus, and attempted to bury her right fist into it. Amine doubled up, gaping like an air-bound goldfish. Zeugma smiled apologetically and turned to the other contest.

For Crow things had gone from bad to worse. Jonathan was demonstrating his mastery of most forms of combat, Oriental and Occidental, and Crow was close to total destruction. Zeugma knew her limitations; her own techniques were fine for disposing of female opposition, but Jonathan could break her neck without quickening his breath. She looked desperately around for a weapon. There was only one possibility, so she used it.

Seizing the brazier by its legs and thrusting it high into the air, she staggered towards the black-robed youth. Amine recovered her breath sufficiently to croak a warning, Jonathan turned from his near-unconscious opponent and screamed in pain and fury as she poured the red-hot charcoal over him.

The initial effect was dramatic, but the respite could only be momentary. Upas danced around, brushing cinders off his robe and out of his hair. Zeugma stooped to urge Crow to his feet, but there was no immediate hope of that. Instead the old man (for now the face seemed creased and lined with many, many years) looked up at her through half-closed eyes and said, 'Flee.'

No one had ever told her to flee before, she thought. It was not a word in common use.

'Flee!' gasped Crow urgently. 'To the centre!'

Behind her she sensed a change of movement. She turned. Upas seemed to have quenched his various conflagrations satisfactorily. Only his eyes still burned, with a flame of vicious, unbridled hatred.

'Flee!' cried Crow.

She fled.

Upas, she surmised later, must have hesitated between pursuit and finishing the work he had started on Crow. Quickly he decided that Crow was no longer a source of worry and in any case Amine was much further on the road to recovery. But the hesitation gave Zeugma a few seconds' start and she was already at the front door when he came out of the room. She vaguely remembered leaving the key in the Range Rover's ignition. She prayed that her memory was true. If she could not get the car started, she was finished. Her head was still muzzy from the fumes and her legs felt weak beyond support of even the most sylph-like frame.

Gasping raucously, she dragged herself into the vehicle and fumbled in panic at the dashboard. She could not even recall where the ignition was. Lights, screen-wipers and radio all went on before her fingers closed on the cool metal of the key. No vampire-pursued Christian ever grasped the protecting crucifix with greater fervour.

Upas was out of the house and almost on her as she turned the key. She sent up a silent blessing to the manufacturers as the engine fired first time. Upas was at the door. She thrust it open with all her strength, hitting him full in the chest and sending him sprawling backwards. Then she found a noisy first gear and the Range Rover pulled away from Upas and danger and horror . . . and Crow.

In the mirror against the light which fell out of the front door, she saw Upas pick himself up and peer after her. His motor-bike stood a few yards away against the side of the house. Would he pursue her or go back inside to finish what he had started with Crow? If he went back inside, Zeugma told herself heavily, she would have to return also. There was no time to go for help, and she could not leave Crow alone. No, it was better by far that Jonathan should pursue her. Amine would almost certainly be able to deal with Crow in his weakened state, but without Jonathan, he might have some kind of chance.

She was now three hundred yards down the drive, almost out of sight of the house. Deliberately she slowed down and switched off the engine, then switched it on and off three times in succession, revving noisily each time. In the ensuing silence she heard the noise she had hoped for. The motor-bike engine bursting into vibrant life. She turned the ignition key once more. It was time to be going. But the engine had grown tired of silly games and merely coughed derisively. She swore angrily and with a fluency she did not know she possessed. This time the engine seemed to realize that the preliminaries were over and the serious business of the night was now beginning. The motor-bike headlights were closing fast and Zeugma was grateful for the degree of acceleration the powerful three-and-a-half-litre engine gave her. Her speed transformed the avenue of beeches into a curving tunnel whose corrugated sides seemed ready at any moment to cave in and crush her, and the drive seemed much longer than she remembered. But at last the two sentinel holly bushes appeared and she let out a sigh of relief as she saw that the gates had remained open.

The Range Rover was good at road-holding in corners, but at speed rather heavy on steering, and Zeugma found her strength taxed to the utmost as she swung the wheel over after only minimal deceleration. Anything else on the road would have to take its chances. In fact anything else on the road would be greeted with joy – it was the road's emptiness up here that bothered her.

The front tyres squealed and she kept up her foot pressure on the accelerator to stop them sliding wide as she wrested the powerful vehicle round on to the narrow thoroughfare. Simultaneously her mind was working out tactics. On the straight she could touch a hundred, but on these roads there were fewer straights than in a game of five card stud. In any case the motor-bike could probably match her for speed and, in the hands of an expert, easily beat her for manoeuvrability. She recalled Jonathan's performance against Twinkle. Of his expertise there could be no doubt.

What was in her favour was that she could make it bloody difficult for him to get by her on these narrow roads, and even if he did the only way he would be able to make her stop was by putting himself and his machine beneath her wheels.

She smiled grimly, quite convinced at that moment of her ability to send the Range Rover's one and three-quarter tons clambering over the highest parts of Master Jonathan Upas.

He was close behind now, weaving and swerving in his efforts to come alongside. Zeugma sent the Rover swaying from side to side, like a dancer responding instinctively to her partner's movements. His headlights moved hypnotically from one side mirror to the other and she could almost sense the frustration of the man as she so easily kept him at bay on the narrow road.

As long as he didn't give up until she got within striking distance of help, she thought. Crow would need all the time she could give him. Though conversely, the longer Upas kept up the chase, the more distant help remained. Twice she had passed farmhouses set well back from the road and not dared risk approaching them in case they should prove empty. Even if she saw a lighted house, the brief moments of exposure as she stopped the car and headed for the door might be enough for Upas. The discovery of her body in a farmyard would still raise the alarm, true; but it might be hours before the trail to the Upases' house would be discovered, by which time they would be long gone.

In any case, Zeugma had a deep-rooted prejudice against ending her life as an anonymous corpse in a midden. A morbid obsession with the place and manner of her death had once troubled her teenage dreams; and she had decided that the *sine qua nons* of mortality were time for a few elegant last words and an appreciative audience. She doubted if Jonathan would provide either.

So it looked as if her best bet was to keep going until she reached a hamlet large enough for a few loud blasts on the horn to bring people to their doors.

Her decision made, she snapped wholly back to the present.

And realized with a shock of mingled relief and dismay that Upas had disappeared. The pursuing headlights showed in none of her mirrors. Had he adandoned the chase so easily? she wondered. She glanced uneasily out of the side window. The road was tortuous here, following the windings of a small stream on her right. Through the dark columns of the trees on the further side, she saw a light moving, dipping, rising, swaying as it followed the rise and fall of the land. It took a few seconds for its significance to sink in.

It was, of course, Upas.

He must have turned off the road, forded the stream and was now racing across country to rejoin the road ahead of her.

Her foot rammed down hard on the accelerator. She was not familiar enough with this road to know how soon its curves would take her in the other direction and deprive Upas of his advantage. But speed was now definitely in her favour. The rough terrain he was crossing must slow him down, negating in some degree the advantage of distance.

And if he should manage to get ahead of her, well, that could be the worst piece of luck he had had all day.

She felt in complete control of the Range Rover now, sending its bulk round the sharper twists and turns of the damp road in a series of well-controlled slides. For a while the motor-bike headlight disappeared and she felt sure she had outrun it; then it was there again, still on the other side of the stream, but slightly ahead now and on an intersection course with the road.

It was going to be close. The next long right-hand curve would be the testing point. She laid the Range Rover into it with all the panache of a Grand Prix driver, had time and confidence enough to see the headlight-illuminated explosion of water as Upas drove his bike through the stream, straightened the wheel as the curve faded out, realized that Upas was, after all, going to make the road ahead of her, and clenched her teeth grimly as she prepared to run him down.

She didn't change her mind. Her mind had nothing to do with it. Something quite non-cerebral in the muscles and sinews of her hands and arms took over, wouldn't let her do what her mind told her was quite essential, and wrenched the wheel round so that the Rover first went into a slide which almost did the job anyway; second, left the road to the left at a speed fatal had rock, tree or bog lain in the way; and third (a reward for virtue? her crystal-clear mind asked) found a rutted, pot-holed, but drivable track which wound uninvitingly uphill into the wilderness of moor and fell which lay on all sides of her.

Zeugma felt no gratitude. To be picking bits of dead Jonathan from the road below was not a very appealing activity; but to be leaving behind her the metalled road which must lead ultimately to society and safety and to have a very live and lethal Jonathan once more in pursuit had even less to commend it. Particularly, she now realized, as the motor-bike and its experienced rider now had all the advantages.

Her only hope now was to keep going. Any stoppage would be fatal. But the track must lead somewhere and as long as she stuck to it and pressed on, there was little Jonathan could do. Dressed in that absurd black robe, he must be feeling pretty cold, she told herself smugly. Eventually he must give up.

But he showed no signs of doing so yet. He was keeping his distance, about twenty yards behind, clearly taking no chances on this uneven surface. She couldn't understand why he seemed so happy to sit back there and wait. It made her uneasy, but there could be no reason . . .

Then ahead she saw the reason.

The track ran through a substantial dry-stone wall. And across the gap was a gate. Five bars it had, of solid construction, fastened to the monolithic wall-end by an iron hoop.

The motor-bike closed up with all the certainty of a kite dropping to a perch by a dying cow. The terrain to the left and right looked uninviting. The only thing to do was what she should have done on the road ten minutes earlier – use the Rover as a battering ram.

Bracing herself against the wheel she sent the vehicle hurtling forward. The bonnet smashed through the central bars; the front wheels rode over the bottom bar and she heard it scraping along the underbody; the windscreen took the full force of the collision with the top bar and Zeugma screamed as the glass crazed and the way ahead disappeared.

Keep the wheel steady, brake gently, punch a hole through the glass: she knew the formula. But road-safety books had not been written with these conditions in mind. The wheel bucked and jerked as the Rover bounced violently over the uneven surface, and she needed both hands to preserve any semblance of control. And to brake meant death.

But this blind driving probably meant death too. She feared that she had left the track. A glance out of the side-window revealed nothing, then the motor-bike headlight ran mockingly over the barren anonymous grassland, filling the rising mist with an eerie luminescence.

It was no use. She slowed, took her right hand off the

wheel and punched at the windscreen. All that happened was that she grazed her knuckles. But a second blow, reminiscent of that one which had disabled Amine, produced a hole about eight inches in diameter.

Three things struck her simultaneously. She was indeed off the track, one of her headlights had been shattered by the collision, and the Range Rover was in trouble.

She was on a steep upslope where the grass was short and very wet and the wheels were beginning to spin. She transferred quickly to the lower gear ratio and managed to keep the forward momentum going, but hovered frequently on the edge of standstill. She glanced desperately round, trying to spot the motor-bike, but its light seemed to have disappeared. Then a figure rose out of the darkness and leapt lightly on to the bonnet. For a second through the ragged hole in the screen she saw Jonathan's face smiling at her, a smile the more hideous because it contained so much of the man's charm. Then the face disappeared as his hand came through the hole and the fingers sought her throat.

She screamed and ducked her head. The grasping fingers caught her hair. She threshed wildly from side to side, lacerating the bare arm against the jags of glass. Blood started up but still he held his grip. Fragments of blood-stained glass broke away and flew into the vehicle as the hole grew bigger.

Zeugma felt the Range Rover coming to a final halt. Still shrieking with pain and terror, she grasped the gear lever and with much crashing and grinding sought and found reverse. The hole in the windscreen was large enough now for Upas to be able to see what he was doing. He forced her head backwards and they looked into each other's eyes. Then he released her hair and his hand slid down to her neck. She revved the engine and let in the clutch. The heavy vehicle plunged blindly back down the slope, the pressure on her throat increased and the misty darkness of the moor began to seep into her head. With a last effort of will, she swung the wheel hard over left and stamped on the brake. For a second the grip on her throat tightened as Upas tried desperately to hang on. Then the hand slipped away, grabbed at the ragged edge of windscreen which fell to pieces instantly, and was gone.

Zeugma was scarcely conscious of what she did now, nor did she know how long had elapsed before the blast of cold wet air through the gaping hole made her aware that she was driving forward once more at a quite insane speed in these conditions.

She slowed. What she could see in the beam of the surviving headlight might have been anywhere within a hundred square miles. The sky was black with cloud preventing even the comfort of a rough direction check. The only thing to be pleased about was the absence of any sign of Upas's motor-bike. Perhaps she had killed him. Or more likely, stunned him and left him to die of exposure. She felt no qualms, would feel nothing except black basic terror until she got off this wilderness.

Ahead something moved in the beam. Her stomach turned at the fear that it might be Upas. But then she sobbed with relief as she saw that it was only a hare. It stood in the light, ears at the alert position and watched her approach with no sign of panic. Only when she got quite close did it turn and lope away. She followed taking some comfort from the sight of a living and non-hostile creature. The hare remained in the beam of light and after a while Zeugma would have been hard put to say whether it was following the twists and turns of the Range Rover or whether she was following it. It didn't seem to matter. Mentally she found she had left the real world, whatever that was, and was drifting along in a state which she recognized as semi-delirium but which she felt no desire to resist. Music began to run through her head. She recognized it as the rapid onward-going theme with which the strings began the last movement of Sibelius' Fifth. It fitted very nicely with her present journey.

Then quite suddenly she knew where she was. The hare had taken a thirty-degree turn to the left and though the terrain seemed outwardly no different from that which she had been covering for the past – how long? ten minutes? hours? days? – she knew beyond doubt that she was on the line of the old Roman Road which ran from the fort at Bewcastle down to Camboglanna. The music now swelled into the majestic final theme. She had a sense of other activity on the road, as though if the mist and darkness would just lift for a moment she would see lines of marching men, and horses straining to haul loaded provision carts up these uncompromising slopes, and hear voices commanding and complaining and cursing their luck, and see behind the faces and the voices to hearts desperate with longing for the heat of a Roman summer or the soft breeze which scarcely moves the spring foliage in the foothills of the Appenines.

Then the hare turned sharply left once more. She followed it up the slope of a ridge, but when the Range Rover reached the crest, the animal had disappeared. But it didn't matter. Below her, black and solid through the mist, was the centre.

The buildings were wrapped in darkness and there was no sign of activity anywhere. But Zeugma had developed a new and uncharacteristic sense of caution in the past hour and now she switched off the Range Rover's engine and freewheeled down to the road. Then, switching off the one surviving headlight, she got out and walked to the gates.

They would be locked, she recalled, and the arrangement made with Lakenheath was that she should blow the car horn. Well, he would just have to respond to her shouts instead.

But when she leaned against the gates, they swung easily open. And now she recalled something else – that

Malcolm Upas had declared his intention of coming here that night.

She hesitated a moment. She had had enough alarms and excitements this evening to last her for two or three lifetimes. The road from the centre to the nearest village was a long one. But it was a real, man-made road and she still had strength enough to walk it. Indeed, she thought, looking back along it and unknowingly echoing Lakenheath's feelings of a couple of hours earlier, it looked a very attractive road, clearly and invitingly signposted to warmth and safety.

But I have promises to keep, she groaned to herself. And besides, surely she had nothing to fear from Malcolm? God knows what he was up to, but at least he didn't seem to share the psychopathic tastes of the rest of the family.

Carefully she slipped through the gates and began a cautious approach to the hospital.

It was as well she did, she realized a few minutes later. The main door of the building was open also and when she stepped inside she heard voices. They seemed to be coming from below and a few moment's search took her to another open door down from which ran a flight of stairs. From the cellar or whatever it was that lay at the bottom came the fitful glow of a naked flame. Someone was talking, a voice she did not recognize. Another responded and this one sounded incredibly, heart-stirringly familiar. Slowly she descended. At the bottom of the stairs was another door, partly ajar. She peered in through the crack.

The first thing she saw in the light of the candle which burnt on top of what looked like a central-heating boiler was Lakenheath. He was sitting on the floor leaning against the boiler and holding a handkerchief to his head. When he took it away, Zeugma saw why. A stream of blood ran down over his ear from a gash in his scalp. He looked pale and drawn and Zeugma found herself biting her tongue to stop crying out at the sight of him. But the next figure she saw put Lakenheath right out of her mind.

Also pale and drawn but with no visible sign of injury on him, there by the boiler stood Leo Pasquino.

Thank God! thank God! said Zeugma inwardly. But the third figure visible to her prevented her from rushing in to the room to express her joy at this longed-for reunion. He had his back to her but she had no difficulty in recognizing him.

It was Diss. And in his hands he carried a shotgun.

There was no point in waiting. The present circumstances were the best she could reasonably hope for. He had his back to her at the moment. If she delayed, he might turn round, even come out and discover her. Or someone else might turn up. Or, most probable of all, sheer terror and the physical aftermath of her recent exertions might paralyse her if she waited and considered.

She pushed the door open. Pasquino and Lakenheath looked up at her. She pressed a finger to her lips but with male stupidity they let their surprise show. Indeed, they went further and spoke.

'My dear,' said Pasquino.

'Oh no,' said Lakenheath.

Diss turned.

Filled with a vast and unsortable variety of angers, she launched herself at him, seizing the barrel of the shotgun and sinking her teeth into the ball of his thumb. He yelled in pain and surprise and the gun fell to the floor. Then, recovering quickly, he tried to shake her off. But she clung tight, wrestling him across the room, shrieking, 'Get the gun! Get the gun!'

She sensed a rapid movement behind her, said a quick prayer of gratitude that one of these stupid men had finally broken free of his paralysis, let herself be thrown free of Diss, and looked up from the floor to see which of them had got the gun.

Pasquino and Lakenheath remained where they had been before. Standing in the middle of the room wielding the weapon with expert menace was Malcolm Upas.

'That was most kind of you, Zeugma,' he said. 'Perhaps you and Mr Diss would now move across and join the others.'

'Nice to see you again, Humpty,' said Pasquino in his most infuriatingly condescending voice.

'When,' asked Lakenheath in tones reminiscent of her old Whitethorn housemistress, 'are you going to learn how to come into a room properly?'

16

*Some apprehended a purifying virtue in
fire, refining the grosser commixture and
firing out the Aethereal particles so deeply
immersed in it.*

'I suppose,' said Zeugma, 'when we get out of this, the
statutory romantic ending requires that we discover we've
loved each other all along, fall passionately into each
other's arms and get married.'

Lakenheath looked at her in alarm and moved away
from her as best as his hog-tied arms and legs would
permit.

'No thanks,' he said. 'I'm not ready for marriage. Far
too immature.'

'Nonsense,' she said firmly. 'You're just prejudiced
against endomorphs. It's merely another facet of your
gross self-conceit.'

'You're wrong,' he said. 'Believe me, I've nothing
against short fat girls. I just happen to prefer long, slim
girls who look elegant at Ascot and who can cross their
legs twice and still have enough left over to fit into a pair
of button-up boots. Pale girls too. I like pale girls, anaemic,
consumptive, corpse-like girls with dark blue shadows
beneath their eyes, and cheek-bones so prominent they
can put your eyes out. That's what I like. You wouldn't
consider a diet, I suppose?'

'Certainly not!' Zeugma exclaimed. 'I'm not fat either.

I'm just plump. But I'm going to get fat, I tell you that. I'm going to eat my way through my husband's bank balance, getting fatter and fatter, so that eventually I may explode. Simultaneously I shall get redder and redder, till the traffic will screech to a halt every time I appear in the street. And I've no intention of ever going near Ascot.'

'That's one consolation, at least,' he answered thoughtfully. 'You mean you'd be a stay-at-home bringing-up-the-kids discover-old-country-recipes kind of wife?'

'Not on your life! I'd be a roam-the-world follow-my-own-career I'm-as-good-as-any-man kind of wife.'

'In that case, perhaps you'd better stick with the professor.'

They fell silent, both very aware of the forced jocularity of the exchange. But it was a source of comfort to them as was the proximity of their bodies which Lakenheath now re-established, rolling back so they lay side by side once more.

'Very touching,' said Jonathan Upas, coming into the boiler house. He had turned up only five minutes after Zeugma, looking she was glad to see, very cold and muddy. But his arrival had made his brother's task much easier.

Zeugma had cursed herself for her impetuousness in attacking Diss, who Lakenheath assured her very confusingly was an American internal security man doing some follow-up work on something called the Healot case.

He had woken up to find that Pasquino had vouched for him and the American was almost apologetic. He and Pasquino were ostensibly on the same side but Lakenheath sensed a kind of tension between the two men. This was explained in part when it emerged that Diss had been assigned to watch over Healot in the States and had lost him on the night he went to his fatal rendezvous with Upas. His interest in recovering the urn and its contents was not merely patriotic; it had to do with reestablishing himself in the shadowy world he inhabited. Pasquino on the other hand only wanted the cash. Yet Lakenheath felt that he was the better bet.

But further revelation of who knew what was prevented by the arrival of Malcolm. And finally and most disastrously, herself.

The reunion with Leo had lacked something of the intense emotionalism with which her imagination had been endowing it over the past few days. His only revealed emotion had seemed to be one of near paternal annoyance that she had got herself into such a scrape.

But the reunion had been shortlived too. Pasquino and Diss had been taken upstairs – a separation of the important from the ignorant, Lakenheath called it as he quickly exchanged stories with Zeugma. Mention of Crow had made his spirits rise for a moment, but Zeugma's description of the man's condition last time she saw him quickly depressed them again. And, though neither put the thought into words, they both realized after their exchange that the Upases would have little desire to see them roaming free and every reason for wishing them dead.

Now Jonathan's entry made both their hearts contract at the thought that perhaps the moment had come.

'What's going on?' asked Lakenheath, trying to appear cool.

Surprisingly Jonathan seemed disposed to answer.

'We're anxious to find out just what those two upstairs know – and of course who else knows it. They're not being very helpful, I'm afraid. Pasquino in particular. It's more difficult with the other; for all we know, he's as pig-ignorant as he looks. But Pasquino, he knows something. He knows where Healot's urn is, for a start. Given time, he would talk. But we're in a hurry and I don't want to risk pushing too hard and killing the poor fool.'

'A humanitarian!' marvelled Lakenheath.

'On the other hand,' grinned Jonathan, 'he may prove

less resistant to pain when it's applied elsewhere. To Miss Gray, for instance. What do you think, Miss Gray?'

Zeugma didn't answer. She couldn't, not without revealing the waves of terror which were beginning to run through her body again. And that, she instinctively sensed, was what Jonathan was looking for.

'What about you, Lakenheath? Do you think you could put up with the lady's screams when a word from you could bring them to a halt?'

Lakenheath looked up at the handsome young man and tried to find the reaction which would give the least pleasure.

'We're all *en route* for death,' he said indifferently. 'So you can make us scream a bit on the way? So what?'

Jonathan bent, undid the bonds round Zeugma's ankles, and dragged her to her feet.

'A stoic, Mr Lakenheath?' he said. 'Well, keep your ears pinned back, as they say.'

At the door Zeugma resisted his pulls and turned back to Lakenheath. Not the tearful farewell, he begged mentally. She spoke. 'Life is just an idiot's delight and as I speed through the dark night into the abyss of oblivion, I can only say thanks, thanks for the memory. Judy Garland. *Babes in Arms.*'

'I thought it was *Little Nellie Kelly*,' he answered. 'In fact, I'm sure it was.'

'No,' her voice drifted back down the stairs. '*Babes in Arms.*'

'Want to bet?' he shouted, but there was no reply.

Now he rolled over and over, wrestling vainly with his bonds, till finally he lay back exhausted and waited for the screaming to start. Their only hope now was Crow. A distant hope, from what Zeugma had told him. But if he could somehow have recovered sufficiently to overcome this formidable female Upas, if he could have summoned help or even got back to the centre himself, if . . .

He heard a footstep on the stairs. Hope and fear clashed in his mind and held his body in a neutral paralysis. A figure appeared at the door, the guttering candle threw out its dying rays then all was darkness. His body slackened, the battle won.

This was not Crow. The final flickers of light had scarcely reached the doorway, but he had seen enough to know that the new arrival was a woman and that in her hand she held a knife.

It must be Amine. Which meant Crow must be dead. Her footsteps were in the room now. They came nearer. The killing was not yet over.

'I thought,' said Zeugma to Jonathan, 'that your sister read longevitude in my palm. *This cow will live for ever,* wasn't that it?'

'You understood? Clever you,' said Jonathan cheerfully. 'Yes, that was it. I have great faith in her perception. I hope she is right. Torturing an immortal used to be a pleasure reserved only for the gods.'

'Jonathan,' said Malcolm harshly. 'Be quiet.'

They were in the old common room where Lakenheath had begun his ill-fated vigil. Someone, Malcolm probably, had brought a couple of oil-lamps and these supplemented the torches to provide a sufficient if rather sinister light. Diss lay against the wall looking very bloody. But his breath came deep and evenly and Zeugma felt that here was a man still to be reckoned with.

Pasquino looked less battered, the result she assumed of the Upases' fear of losing him rather than of any special compassion.

'Hasan,' she said. He turned and looked at her but she could find no more to say. She saw him still as the man she had known in Cairo; civilized, amusing, attentive; her lover. A few words overheard at his house; they could mean anything. A garbled story of blackmail and intrigue second or third hand from Lakenheath; he could have got it all wrong.

'Hasan,' she said. 'What's happening? Why don't you stop all this nonsense and . . .'

Her Whitethorn scolding voice died away as she heard it and recognized its absurdity. 'All this nonsense' was Pasquino in chains, Diss's blood-caked face in the lamplight, Lakenheath lying in bonds below, his cousin and her friends killed with an obscenity her own recent experience let her imagine fully, Crow crumpled and broken in a smoke-filled room, Healot swinging by his neck in an aseptic anonymous American hotel room. That was 'all this nonsense'; and all the good common sense and all the sympathetic reasoning of all the rational, wordly wise schoolmistresses in the world could never put Humpty together again.

Malcolm nodded as if reading her thoughts and agreeing with her conclusions.

'Forget everything, Zeugma,' he said. 'No appeals to the past. Just concentrate on getting Leo to talk, then we can all go home.'

'Home?'

'Why, yes.' He sounded surprised. 'Once we lay our hands on Healot's urn, that's it. Off we go, back to the sun and the sand, you wriggle out of your bonds and give the local constabulary a thrill and we can have a laugh together about all this in the Cairo Hilton by midsummer.'

Zeugma was taken aback by the charming effrontery of this.

'People have been killed,' she said. 'Sayer, Healot. Probably Crow. How do you imagine we could ever laugh together again?'

'Good girl,' said Diss. 'You tell the bastard. Ah!'

He cried out as Jonathan side-footed him in the groin. Malcolm shrugged indifferently.

'Let me put it another way,' he said, 'Leo, unless you

tell us where in your estimation the urn is hidden, I'll turn Jonathan loose on Zeugma.'

Pasquino looked from one face to another. Something he saw in Jonathan's must have decided him.

'It's only a theory you understand,' he said wearily. 'Healot said something about Pharaoh's tomb. It might be just a figure of speech, meaningless. But the only spot round here to resemble an Egyptian tomb is one of the fuel silos.'

'What?' Malcolm grabbed excitedly at the large-scale plan of the centre which lay on the floor. 'The silos. Of course. But how . . . ? The pipes were concreted over, surely. He would not leave it where he could not get at it, would he?'

'Why not?' asked Jonathan. 'It was the knowledge that he had it which he believed to be his strength.'

'No. His was not that kind of mind,' said Malcolm. 'If it is there, it's retrievable.'

He pored over the plan once more.

'Here's something. But what . . . that fellow, Lakenheath, he must know this place well. Get him up here!'

Jonathan moved to the door, but Diss interrupted him.

'Don't bother,' he said in resigned tones. 'When they build silos like these, they need to be able to get into them for inspection and maintenance from time to time. There must have been tunnels to the inspection hatches as well as flow pipes.'

So, thought Zeugma, looking scornfully at Diss, the American's appearance of strength and fortitude was delusive. He believed something could be bought by appeasement, the common error of statesmen in the face of thugs.

'Yes. This dotted line . . . but has it too been concreted over? Jonathan, watch these people. Just *watch*!'

Malcolm left, carrying the plan and Jonathan drove Zeugma against the wall with the shotgun.

'If the urn is there,' asked Diss, 'what are you going to do with us?'

'Oh stop whining!' snapped Zeugma. 'He's going to kill us, can't you see? And in the nastiest way possible, if he has any choice.

'To travel painfully is better than to arrive,' mocked Jonathan. 'A little accident will occur. A fire. Mr Lakenheath's obsession with this place is well known to the police. You drop him here, go back to pick him up after a pleasant evening with your friends. The professor insists that he accompanies you, concerned as he is for your safety. And then, the accident!'

'This place won't burn easily!' said Pasquino confidently.

'Help has been arranged,' said Jonathan.

'And what about me?' asked Diss.

'You are nothing,' said Jonathan. 'You will remain nothing and no one will notice whether you move or are still. Perhaps I will give you to my sister.'

He paused after mentioning Amine and his face became still, as though listening for some remote sound to be repeated.

Behind him the door slowly opened, creaking slightly. It seemed impossible for Jonathan not to hear, but it seemed that what he was listening for was more distant than the door and the figure who now appeared was able to enter the room undetected.

Zeugma recognized her with a shock of disbelief.

It was Miss Peat and in her hands she clutched Lakenheath's walking stick.

It seemed imperative to try to cover the sound of her approach.

'What makes you think Amine's in a fit state to want him?' demanded Zeugma.

But the words were counter-productive. Jonathan snapped back to here and now, looked at her enquiringly for a second; Miss Peat took another step and, warned either by his ears or something in Zeugma's face, Jonathan spun round with the shotgun levelled. The woman was

198

still well out of attacking range, but she tried. She flung the stick forward, Upas parried it easily with the shotgun barrel and laughed. Then Diss rolled himself from the wall with all the strength he could muster and scythed his legs viciously against Jonathan's calves.

The young man kicked his feet in the air like a chorus girl and tumbled backwards, still clutching the gun. But he was lithe as a cat and rolled sideways avoiding with ease Miss Peat's desperate dive. It looked as if the battle was still going to go his way.

So Zeugma kicked him at the base of the neck. Fortunately she had not come to Cumberland prepared for much socializing and the shoes she wore were solid and sensible rather than flimsy and frivolous. And she had a good kick. Jonathan subsided with a pleasantly rattling groan and Miss Peat plucked the shotgun from his unresisting fingers.

'You took your time,' accused Diss.

'Sorry,' said Miss Peat. 'I went to the cellar first. But there was only Lakenheath there, and he couldn't come upstairs with me without rousing the whole county.'

She put the shotgun down and produced a knife.

'Turn round, my dear, and we'll get you loose,' she said to Zeugma. Her whole manner of talking and moving had changed; the vegetable slowness of her previous appearances had disappeared entirely.

'You knew she was coming?' said Zeugma to Diss. 'So that's why you told Malcolm about the inspection tunnel.'

'That's it,' said Diss. 'Also, if he's foolish enough to open up any of those hatches without proper breathing apparatus, he's got a surprise coming. There should be enough vapour still hanging around in there to give him a nasty moment.'

Zeugma's bonds were almost loose when there was a movement at the door. She turned and saw it was Lakenheath standing there. She smiled broadly at him, recalling their last conversation and feeling a new bond between them. But her smile froze as some unseen force suddenly thrust him into the room, sending him crashing to the floor.

Behind him stood Malcolm, clutching the torch he had just struck Lakenheath with. Miss Peat bent for the shotgun as Jonathan came to life and launched himself at her legs in a rugby tackle which brought her to the floor. Lakenheath meanwhile had found sufficient strength to get back to his feet and was grappling with Malcolm in the doorway. It was a brave but doomed effort. Lakenheath's ankle had been under too much strain already that night and though he hopped around on the other foot with all the agility of a Long John Silver, it was no contest. But he hung on tenaciously taking a vast amount of punishment in his efforts to keep Malcolm from the shotgun.

The shotgun. That was the key, Zeugma realized. Who would get there first. Peat or Jonathan? Malcolm or Lakenheath?

Or herself. The loosened ropes finally parted at her wrists and she was free. Peat was doing a good job of anchoring the still dazed Jonathan to the floor, but Lakenheath, though still draped round Malcolm's neck, was being bludgeoned into insensibility.

Zeugma stooped and picked up the shotgun. Hunting, shooting and fishing had been available at Whitethorn, but a girl who felt as menaced as she did could never derive any pleasure from slaughtering the uncomprehending and the defenceless. But Malcolm was neither of these and she levelled the gun with as much assumption of expertise as she could muster.

'Stop it,' she said. '*Stop it!*'

Malcolm and Lakenheath looked at her together and the latter, realizing that he made a large part of a communal target, released his grip and stepped back.

'Thanks,' he said, 'but I was wearing him down.'

Then he subsided gently to the floor.

Malcolm took a step towards her.

'No,' she said.

'Zeugma, listen to me,' he said reasonably. 'It's all over. All I want to do now is go in peace. This American's right. I nearly choked when I opened that inspection hatch. If the urn's in there, then we cannot get it, not without equipment. So I'm pulling out. Will you let me go?'

'I don't think I can do that, Hasan,' she said.

'Why not? It's a big world. And there are worse people in it than me.'

'Name six,' she said.

'I was your first lover,' he said seriously. 'I remember our days together with tenderness. This is no way for such a thing to end. Let me go.'

He moved towards her and she found herself against her will and intention retreating before him.

'Can you shoot me? No, I think not. Put up the gun, Zeugma. It's all over. No one is much harmed. Put up the gun and we will go.'

She was now back against the wall. She was dimly aware that the Peat–Jonathan bout had been suspended and the contestants while keeping a tight hold of each other were watching the main confrontation as keenly as the others.

Lakenheath was trying to push himself off the floor to return to the fray.

'Don't listen,' he mumbled through bloody lips.

'Zeugma, be careful!' urged Pasquino.

'Blow his bloody head off!' pleaded Diss.

But she felt helpless, paralysed, as Malcolm slowly approached, a friendly smile on his lips, hand outstretched for the weapon which seemed to pull with increasing weight against her arm muscles.

'Give me the gun, Zeugma,' repeated Malcolm.

She ought to shoot. She knew she ought to shoot. But

she did not know how anyone ever found the strength of hatred to press a trigger and send another human being spinning off into the emptiness beyond.

'The gun, Zeugma.'

'Zeugma, my love,' said Pasquino rapidly, urgently. 'Forgive me. This man is evil. Many good men have died because of him. Many. Your father among them. He didn't drown by accident. He killed himself because this man . . .'

Zeugma did not hear the rest. She saw the change on Malcolm's face, saw him hesitate in his advance, saw him step back and begin to retreat in the face of her own new expression.

'No,' he said. 'No.'

Jonathan took Miss Peat by surprise, threw her from him and rushed at Zeugma. She saw him coming but did not change her aim. Carefully she squeezed the trigger.

'Hasan!' screamed Jonathan.

But he was calling to someone who was no longer there.

For a moment he knelt on one knee by his brother's body. Then he rose, stared white-faced at Zeugma, and said, 'You shall know me.'

And, seizing the table with both hands, he overturned it, shattering the oil lamps and sending trickles of liquid flames running over the wooden floor.

After that it was chaos. Zeugma and Miss Peat struggled desperately to untie the two captives while Lakenheath beat his jacket vainly against the flames. Jonathan meanwhile had disappeared, but that he had not instantly fled from the centre was apparent when Zeugma helped Pasquino to his feet and saw that the door was blocked by a wall of fire. Through the windows she saw that flames were beginning to burgeon all over the centre. Lines of fire were running along the corridors of the quadrangle buildings with a speed that indicated that Jonathan's talk of burning the place down had been no idle threat. Only trails of paraffin could explain the rapidity with which the fire was spreading.

They would have to escape by the windows and this proved more difficult than Zeugma anticipated. Sayer in his post-hippy enthusiasm for security had had them all fitted with internal padlocks and Lakenheath's master-keys were not intended to open these. Finally and with great difficulty they smashed the glass and were almost roasted in the upsurge of flame caused by the night air rushing in.

As they clambered out, Zeugma thought she heard the noise of Jonathan's motor-bike, but she could not be sure.

Diss was helping Pasquino, and she and Miss Peat supported Lakenheath, despite his protestations of strength and vitality. They made for the main gate which was flanked now by tall pillars of flame from the buildings on either side.

'Like hell-mouth,' said Lakenheath as they approached. 'Abandon hope.'

'But we're going out,' rejoined Zeugma.

Moments later they were through and at the Range Rover into which they all climbed with great relief, though Pasquino looked a little put out when he saw the shattered windscreen.

'You drive too fast,' he said reproachfully.

'My car's tucked out of sight just off the road,' said Diss.

'May I offer you a lift?' asked Zeugma formally.

'I'd appreciate it.'

'Look,' said Miss Peat.

They followed the direction indicated by her out-stretched hand.

The centre was now a solid square of flame and the light this cast touched the heights of the ridge from which Lakenheath had overlooked the buildings two days earlier.

Someone was up there. No, Zeugma realized. Two people.

'Who the hell's that?' asked Diss.

'Let's take a look,' said Zeugma.

She sent the Range Rover bumping up the gully which led to the track below the ridge. Pasquino drew in his breath in amazed disbelief when he realized that only one headlight worked, but he did not speak. When Zeugma reached the foot of the ridge, she stopped and climbed out. From here the centre itself was not visible but the glow in the sky formed a bright backcloth to the figures silhouetted on the crest above. She had known who they were as soon as Peat had pointed them out, but this close confirmation filled her heart with relief and concern.

Without speaking to the others, she began to scramble up to where Jonathan and Crow confronted each other above the blazing centre.

'Hang on. What happened to Florence Nightingale?' complained Lakenheath. She turned, took his reaching hand and began to help him up the slope. He had a right to be there too.

As though sensing this, the others remained by the Rover.

Above, the two men had joined in a desperate struggle all the fiercer for being conducted in almost complete silence. Crow had thrown his long sinewy arms around his younger opponent and locked his hands together in the Cumberland wrestling style at which he was so expert. Jonathan subscribed to no particular style but was ready to launch attacks with fists, feet, elbows, knees, teeth – anything at his disposal. All Crow seemed to be doing was holding on, and from the brief glimpses Zeugma got as she made her way up the slope at Lakenheath's slow pace, it sometimes appeared to her as if the form and size of Jonathan had changed within that formidable circlet of arms. Sometimes Crow seemed to be wrestling with a creature of great bulk and ferocity, at others it was as if his arms were wrapped round nothing

204

at all. It was an illusion, Zeugma decided, caused by the uncertain light and the rapid foot movements of the pair as their struggles forced them to and fro along the ridge. At times they descended towards Zeugma, at others they sank almost out of sight down the other side. But always Crow's grip held and the struggles of Jonathan began to smack less of fury and more of despair.

Finally, inevitably, as Zeugma helped Lakenheath up the last steep section, the young man's body slackened and, still bound by those relentless arms, he sank to his knees on the damp coarse grass which their feet had trampled almost to mud.

Crow held him still for a moment then unclasped his arms.

'You have defiled this ancient earth,' he said. 'Go now. Leave it, if you can.'

Jonathan almost fell as the supporting arms let him go. Then he rose, his body wrapped in a sinister miasma of perspiration, and rushed down the slope a few paces to where his motor-bike lay.

'You can't let him go!' cried Zeugma as he started the machine.

'Wait,' commanded Lakenheath, holding her back.

Jonathan pointed the machine down the slope towards the flaming centre. There were no farewell dramatics from him; every instinct of his body cried out for flight.

Even in her anger at his escape, Zeugma had once again to admire the grace and authority of his riding. So might some young priest have escaped astride a dolphin from the monstrous catacylsm that engulfed Atlantis, she thought as she watched his progress north along the burning perimeter of the centre.

'Crow,' she said. 'Are you hurt? What happened to Amine?'

'I could not help,' he answered strangely. 'Outside the circle, she was lost.'

Zeugma opened her mouth to ask another question, but

a strange noise like a grumbling in the earth interrupted her. Then the ground beneath her feet seemed to shudder.

'Look!' said Lakenheath.

Below them an area of ground on the west side of the centre was in turmoil. The coarse-grassed turf of the waste seethed and stirred like some turgid liquid coming to the boil in a cauldron.

Jonathan was on the fringe of the disturbance and, standing high on the footrests, he rode it like a surfer in turbulent seas. It was hard not to feel an impulse to applaud as he gained the safety of solid ground. But now came a second grumbling and again the earth stirred. This time he seemed to be in the middle of it.

'What's happening?' screamed Zeugma.

'My God!' It was Diss who had come scrambling up the slope, closely followed by the others as the earth-tremors reached them. 'It's the fuel silos. The fire must have got to the inspection tunnel and the vapour's going up.'

Once again Jonathan was performing the impossible, urging the bike forward as the ground bubbled up and fell away beneath his wheels. Once again he made it and this time he pointed the machine due west, away from the centre and into the red-tinged mist which modulated into blackness and safety. But there was no path for him that way. A shape ran from the mist – was it Twinkle? It had to be Twinkle; but there were other shapes there too, it seemed to Zeugma, some on the ground, some in the air, changed, corrupted, perhaps even created by the deceiving vapours. Whatever their reality, Jonathan changed his course, heading north and parallel to the centre once more.

And now came the final tremor, longer and more violent than the others.

This time there was no escape. The earth did not bubble, it opened. One moment Jonathan was there, a man, living and striving for life, next he was gone.

Then the earth was still and only the crackling of the centre fire which also seemed to be failing disturbed the night silence.

Without speaking they all descended from the ridge, all except Crow, who stood there clutching what looked like a small branch stripped from a tree.

When they reached the hole into which Jonathan had plunged, they halted. It was deep but the flames let them see to the bottom. There was no sign of his body, though a wheel of the motor-bike protruded from the broken earth and still spun silently.

Zeugma turned away and put her arms round Pasquino, seeking comfort and forgetfulness. He pressed her to him.

'Well, if Healot left his urn down there, it'll be shattered to oblivion now,' said Diss.

'Yes,' said Pasquino. 'But, I say, now that looks interesting. Excuse me, my dear. Let me have that torch, will you Miss Peat?'

Disengaging himself from Zeugma, he descended into the hole and, on his knees, began to brush the earth away from a fragment of stone which the upheaval had left on the surface.

'This *is* interesting,' he said with enthusiasm. 'Zeugma, take a look at this. By heaven, it's going to be worth going over this area very carefully. Very carefully indeed. It's an ill wind and all that.'

Zeugma turned from the pit and began to walk away. A few yards behind her stood Lakenheath, who regarded her with an expression of sad sympathy which he tried to disguise as she walked past him.

'You were right,' he said. 'It was *Babes in Arms*.'

She didn't even pause.

'You can go to hell too,' she said over her shoulder.

He watched her disappear back towards the ridge and after a while slowly began to follow.

17

But the long habit of living indisposeth us for dying.

It had rained all night, but with Utopian timing the showers had died away at dawn, and now halfway through the morning the clouds were mere outcrops of puffballs on a rich blue ground. It was possible to believe in summer once more.

Zeugma looked down from her vantage point above the centre and wondered how long it would be before the landscape assimilated these modern ruins as thoroughly as it had done the Romans'. Barely a fortnight had passed since the fire and already wind had scattered the finest ashes and rain had bound together what remained and the tough, irrepressible moor grasses were sinking roots in this strange compost.

The police had gone and the press had retreated, leaving a few outriders in the bars of Brampton. Official noises, both soothing and warning, had kept the story within limits, though these themselves were sensational enough. There had been inquests. The Upas brothers' deaths had been declared accidental. 'What they had been doing in the deserted centre we do not know and perhaps it is better that we do not know', said the coroner sternly. 'But it may be something of a poetic justice that they themselves caused the fire which killed them.'

This strong hint accompanying a verdict of murder in

the inquest on the exhumed bodies of Lakenheath's cousin and her friends gave everybody much cause for speculation. The police declaration that they considered both cases closed confirmed the connection. The part played by Zeugma and the others had never been mentioned.

The subterranean explosions had caused some interest and concern among experts who had been amazed at their violence. Jonathan's body, though not visible on the night of the event, had been found lying on the surface the following morning as though the earth had rejected it. Now the hollow had a canvas shelter over part of it and drainage trenches radiated from its lowest corners as Pasquino sifted through the disturbed soil with obsessive enthusiasm.

Zeugma turned away and strode energetically across the waste, her gum-boots kicking up fountains of water-drops from the tussocks of grass. After recent events, this landscape ought to have been unbearably sinister to her, she thought. But somehow it was not so. On the contrary, today it felt like a holy and blessed place, gentle swells of earth, grass and rock running away to horizons against which time and mutability scratched in vain. Inside these invisible limits, whatever is, or had been, or would be, existed together without the conflicts called progress or history. She began to sing and wild creatures all around ceased what they were doing to listen, amazed. It was her old school song, she realized. Suddenly for the first time in her life its rhetorical optimism made sense.

She was in a more subdued mood when she reached Crow's cottage, for she now realized, that, unawares, she had made a decision.

She knocked at the door. There was no answer so she pushed it open. As on her last visit here, she sensed life within but this time she was determined not to be startled and her entrance was ultra-cautious.

'Boo!' said a voice, and she jumped in fright.

Sitting by the fireplace with one of Crow's drinking bowls in his hand was Lakenheath.

'Aren't you coming in?' he asked.

'Yes. Of course. I came to see Crow,' she explained annoyed with herself.

'I didn't expect that you'd come to see me,' said Lakenheath.

Indeed, they had seen very little of each other since the night of the fire, and when they had met, the circumstances had never been conducive to private conversation. Zeugma had seen him at the inquest on Julie and the sight of his white strained face had touched her more deeply than almost anything else that had happened.

Now he looked much better and his ankle resting on a cushion of peat turves before the hearth, looked as if its proportions were back to normal.

'What do you want with Crow?' he asked, as she sat down at the other side of the hearth.

'I came to say goodbye,' she said. 'No, that's not true, really. I just set out to see him, but on my way here I realized I was coming to say goodbye.'

'So you're going. Well, well. Has the greatest archaeologist in the world decided to go and discover Atlantis then?'

She ignored the gibe.

'No. Leo's staying. They think he's looking for bits of Healot's urn in that hole, but he's not. He reckons he's found a fragment of the gnomon from the sundial on the Bewcastle Cross. I think he hopes the actual cross-piece itself may turn up. After that he's still got his Solway Firth project, so he could be around for quite a time.'

'But you are going,' he repeated.

'Yes,' she said. He asked for no explanation and she was glad. The best she could have offered was that at twenty-five even short fat girls no longer needed guardians. Or more honestly perhaps that when Leo had told her the truth about her father's death, the only thing he had been guarding her against had disappeared, and she had since realized that he could offer her no other kinds of protection.

'What about you?' she asked.

'Me. Oh, I'm going too,' he answered. 'I can hardly stay on, can I? Even if the office weren't going to fold up, which it is. It was just a front, you see. A nice easy way of keeping an eye on parties interested in the centre. That's why I got the job. They didn't want anyone good and experienced enough to see that it was a load of nothing. Just a figurehead with Miss Peat really running matters. She knew I'd made up Diss and Charnell Bearings, of course. But they weren't quite sure why. So when that American hatchet-man expressed an interest, she suggested he should call himself Diss to stir me up a bit.'

'And Sayer?'

'Yes, he was real. Poor bastard. He'd fallen out with the *real* Cumberland Development Council people and been the perfect authentic backer for the N.E.C.D.C. An unfortunate casualty, said Peat. I told her to get stuffed. That's one advantage of having your employee become your boss. You can tell him or her to get stuffed!'

Zeugma poked the peat fire. Outside the air was full of spring warmth, but it took more than a few hours of April sunshine to penetrate these thick stone walls.

'You're a bit like me,' she said diffidently. 'You've found you're rather less important than you thought.'

'What?' he said indignantly, then laughed. 'I suppose so. Though I did do quite well in the circumstances. Do you know, Peat didn't send half my stuff out? Needless expense, she said, and in any case, they didn't want too many people tramping around and blurring the picture! And guess who turned up yesterday. Bulstrode! Yes, the Poly-fibre man. Not about a factory, but he had been doing some financial research into turning Blackrigg and one or two other places into holiday dormer villages. You recall he mentioned this in the Old Kith the first time we met? So I wasn't a total failure, was I?'

It was Zeugma's turn to be indignant.

'That fat slob! Yes, I remember him. What did you say?'

'Well, I am out of a job,' said Lakenheath slowly. 'And there could be a lot of money in the scheme. And I do like it up here. So . . .'

'So . . . ?' Her voice was vibrant with menace.

'I took a leaf out of the Upas book, told him I'd kept a close eye on him and his Miss Amis, even taken a few snaps, and if I ever heard his name mentioned again in this area, I'd be in touch with his wife. That did the trick. But it's funny, I felt bad about it afterwards. It's not a long step to being a Upas, is it? Malcolm, I mean. Not those other two perverts.'

Zeugma didn't answer, and Lakenheath looked at her curiously.

'You were close to Malcolm once, I gather. I was surprised . . .'

'Why?'

'I don't know. I thought of you as, well, sort of . . .'

'Inexperienced?' she snapped. 'Not many people's cup of tea?'

'No,' he said gently. 'Not inexperienced. Innocent, that's nearer to it. As though you were still waiting for the world to arrive.'

'It must be something to do with good healthy flesh,' she answered. 'You can't spot the scar tissue so easily as in skinny people. Talking of which, whatever happened to Amine, I wonder.'

'There was no trace of her at the house,' said Lakenheath.

'I know. I wondered if Crow had said anything to you.'

'No. Just that there was a struggle. But he didn't say who between.'

Zeugma looked at him quizzically and shook her head.

'You're quite gone on all this magic bit, aren't you?' she said.

'I lack your calm rationality, perhaps,' he answered. 'Things happen. I don't always understand them, that's all. What about your own experiences in that house?'

'Hallucinations,' she answered promptly. 'Something they burnt gave off fumes that got to me.'

'And Crow's fight with Jonathan? And the way that he died.'

'It was just a wrestling match. We were out of breath, distraught, it was dark. As for the earth opening up and swallowing him, that was just the fuel silos going up.'

'They were empty.'

'Vapour hangs on. You told me yourself. That's why they sealed them up.'

'Malcolm said he'd only opened one. And the scientific boys who came up last week can't understand the way the earth moved.'

'The heat from the fire must have cracked the doors on the others. Look, you can't really believe any of this, can you? It's not even as if there's any kind of recognizable pattern. There's bits of everything, medieval magical lore, Stone Age burial rites, Mithraic sacrifices, Nordic earth-mother stuff; I mean it's a mish-mash, a bit of everything from abracadabra to Aleister Crowley!'

'You know,' said Lakenheath with a grin, 'if you don't believe in it, you can hardly demand consistency from it, can you?'

Zeugma shook her head in exasperation. Feeling strangely unsettled she got up and went to the open door. There was no sign of Crow though high in the sky to the west she could see a soaring black cross which may have been his falcon.

'I think perhaps I'll go,' she said.

'Without saying goodbye?'

213

'You can say it for me when he gets back.'

'I mean, to me,' said Lakenheath. 'You *were* going to come and see me too, weren't you?'

'Yes, I suppose so. I don't know,' admitted Zeugma, then suddenly, surprising herself, she asked, 'Why were you discharged from the army?'

'Good Lord!' he said. 'Which of my two stories would you prefer? The one about the sergeants' mess fund, or the one about being shot through the kneecap in Aden?'

She thought for a moment.

'You don't have much luck with your legs,' she said finally.

'No. I don't suppose I do. Lucky with love, unlucky with legs. Though it doesn't bother me much, and my ankle's back to normal. Crow bakes a marvellous poultice.'

'Muttering spells as he does it, I've no doubt,' she said sarcastically.

'Perhaps. Look, if you've decided to leave your professional mole to his burrowings and you've not yet decided when to go, what's the hurry? Believe it or not, I sometimes get very tired of my own company. You'd do me a favour, not to say an honour, if you'd sit down and chat till Crow comes.'

Zeugma looked at him, trying to detect mockery either in his face or in his voice. There was none and she smiled, not knowing that her smile was a luminous, joyful thing which had always weighed mightily in the balance against the bitchiness, belligerence and impetuosity of her career at Whitethorn and subsequently in the world at large.

'All right,' she said.

'Great. Then have a drink.'

'What are you drinking?' she said.

'One of Crow's concoctions. He seems to believe it has some efficacy as a love-potion.'

'Really?' she asked. 'And is it working?'

'I'm not quite sure. Why not try some yourself?'
'All right,' she said.
And she sat down and drank.

Out on the moor, Crow paused beneath the mighty April sky. A rare smile touched his lips and Twinkle came up and rubbed against his sinewy legs.

Through his mind now passed all the images which had come to him on that uneasy winter's night. All had now surfaced in that unimportant tributary which men call time. All except one, the picture of himself buried deep in some cavern from which only his despairing cries could hope to escape.

He held that one before him thoughtfully for a while. Perhaps it was still to come. Perhaps it had been already, long long ago.

No matter. He shook his head and let the image dissolve.

Twinkle moved ahead, looked back, and barked once impatiently.

Crow turned towards him, glanced sunwards with unhooded eyes to confirm his direction and with long easy strides began once more to trace the great mysterious lines of power which are the sinews of the living earth.

MYSTERY
Hill

Hill, Reginald

Beyond the bone

DUE DATE
